COYOTE

Charles Combee

WolfSinger Publications ∫ Security, Colorado

Map Artwork by Irina Combee

Cover Art copyright 2022 © Carol Hightshoe
Cover Layout by Carol Hightshoe

ISBN 978-1-944637-29-3

Printed and bound in the United States of America

PROLOGUE

I slid around the corner of the building, breathing in hushed bursts. I convulsed as I tried to silence my breath, tried to minimize every sound I made. I wanted to disappear, to become a breath of wind, silently sighing as I made my way along.

I felt the sweat trickle down the side of my face, partly from exertion, the remainder a product of fear. Bile rose in my throat and the acrid mixture forced a sharp cough as I drew it into my lungs.

So much for silently sighing.

The parking garage was dimly lit, and I was able to merge into the dark shadow of night rather well, although I regretted the shirt. It was light blue, a color I favored, but not right now. The shirt gathered shards of light from the surrounding air and fluoresced, a small patch of pale blue beckoning from the surrounding gloom.

I waited, straining to hear. You know, it's funny how you know that you can't improve your hearing by exerting yourself, but you can't help it, you have to try.

Especially in times like these.

My breathing slowed, and I wasn't gulping for air anymore. As I felt my breathing even out, I relaxed a little bit. I convinced myself he hadn't seen me after all. I was actually beginning to think I was going to make it. That I could escape.

I waited a few minutes more, just to be safe and gingerly stepped away from the wall, stepping lightly, noiselessly. I sidled down the passage, keeping the wall close, and I maintained contact with it, brushing my left hand lightly down it as I moved towards the corner.

The air noticeably brightened as I advanced, and soon I was at the corner. This is where the lightly used hallway merged into the regular confines of the garage, and I stopped, considering my next move. I knew I couldn't stay here forever. I needed to move on, to get out of the parking area and into the apartments above.

I sighed softly and steeled myself. I poked my head out briefly, making sure to minimize the time my head would be visible. I didn't see anything, just the dull gray driveway slanting upwards to my left. I hesitated. I still didn't see anything. The garage was deserted. It felt as if it were ripped from our universe and was deposited on the farthest shore of time and space. The desolation, the loneliness, was palpable. I took this as a good sign and moved slowly forward out into the light.

I took a few steps when I heard a strange noise. It was a clicking, a sharp noise that burst towards me in a staccato that shattered my sense of relief, my fear returned in a rush that created a wrenching sensation through my whole body. I was frozen, unable to move, and any chance of escape became irrelevant.

The clicking soon transposed itself into the reality of a set of two hairy feet ending in sharp claws. The feet were canine in basic shape and form, and the only aspect of them that was abnormal was that the creature strode on them upright. Coyote was striding towards me, a casual maelstrom of power and malevolence.

I froze, indecisive. No use running. He would just catch me anyway.

"What do you want?" I barked. "How did you find me here?"

Coyote stepped softly towards me, stopped, just out of reach. He was clad in the same outfit as before. A red blazer and bowler hat, strangely incongruous, both were worn as if they were part of a designer outfit. He didn't have the ivory pipe though. His eyes caught mine, and they gleamed with a feral ferocity only matched by his intelligence.

"Do you have any idea what you've done?" he inquired softly. "Now I'm going to have to wake up, again. I haven't been awake, not really, not for a long, long time."

I stared at him, a strange mixture of stark terror and curiosity running through me, chilling the marrow of my bones.

"What are you?" I managed to blurt out. "What were you doing down in that canyon? I've never seen anything like it before."

"You're never going to see anything like it again," he responded quietly. "You weren't meant to see that. It is for us, not you. Humans aren't allowed, aren't supposed to know."

"What are you talking about?" I demanded. "Why wasn't I meant to see it? What do you mean when you say, "wake up"? You were awake that night, weren't you?"

Coyote grinned at me. "You'll find out," he responded calmly. "All things will be clear. You'll understand what you've done. One more thing," he added. "Don't come back to the canyon, ever."

He bared his teeth at me in a garish caricature of a smile and gave a short bark. He took his hat in hand and bowed to me, a gesture both mocking and derisive.

I felt a rush of anger hit me. I literally saw red, and a quintessential moment passed over me. I lost control of my emotions, which I rarely do, and the finely balanced scale between fight or flight crumbled, landing squarely on the side of fight.

I rushed him, and while my plan wasn't really thought through very well, the basic idea was good. I hoped to deliver a crushing blow and disable his main weaponry, a mouthful of baleful, extremely sharp teeth.

As I closed within arm's reach, I delivered a slap to the side of his head...or what I took to be his head. My arm sliced through empty air, and I panicked as I lost my balance and tumbled to the cement floor. I rolled and came up ready. I'm a brown belt in a Philippine martial art known as Arnis, so I recovered very quickly and raised my arms in a defensive stance.

Nothing. Coyote was gone, vanishing into thin air like a wisp of steam, gently losing cohesion and fading away like the last breath of light on a winter's day. The space was too open to account for his abrupt disappearance. I moved a couple of steps over to where he had been standing a couple of seconds before. I thought I might find a couple of claw marks in the paint on the floor. I investigated all around me carefully, but there was nothing. Instinctively, I sniffed the air. A faint smell of...something. It was a raw, pungent odor that elicited a feeling of the primeval forest.

I shook my head, trying to clear the funny smell. The garage was empty. I was shaken and afraid. I stood; my mind aflame with one burning question. How had this creature found me?

I gave up on finding him and slowly headed upstairs to my apartment. I unlocked the door and cautiously entered. It seemed like my normal, regular, reassuring living room. Nothing was out of place, and I didn't see any evidence anyone had visited. Maybe I was being paranoid but seeing Coyote downstairs had given me the creeps.

I tossed my jacket on the back of the couch and headed to kitchen to make some coffee. I always like coffee in the evening; I find it somehow completes the day.

I was nearly to the fridge; actually extending my arm to grab the handle, when I suddenly paused. A faint aroma wafted its way into my nostrils, insinuating its way into my conscious. I recognized the smell from downstairs in the garage. I hesitated and turned, whirled, and ran into the bedroom. I touched my finger to the safe I keep on the dresser. It sprang open, and I grabbed my handgun. I knew it didn't help the last time, but it gave me the feeling of security I needed, here and now.

I crept back into the living area and searched the whole apartment carefully. I opened all the closet doors and returned to the bedroom. I steeled myself and crouched down quickly, checking under the bed. After all, Coyote might make a perfect monster to terrorize young children. The only thing I saw was a reminder I should vacuum once in a while.

Resting easier now, I returned to the kitchen and made my coffee. I kept the gun with me, though. The whole experience had really unsettled me, and I needed the pistol, a security blanket that allowed me to push back the thoughts that assailed my peace of mind, as if a piece of metal could somehow banish the monster in the closet and shine a light on the dark corners where evil dwells.

A few hours later, I crawled into bed. I tossed and turned for a bit, brief visions of Coyote suddenly stepping out of the closet, assailing me, these thoughts nipping every chance of dropping off to sleep like a Blue Heeler hard on the heels of an unfortunate cow. These thoughts whirled for a bit, but my mind finally cleared, and I drifted off to sleep.

~ * ~

The ancient man was carefully making his way along a trail that threaded along the edge of a steep cliff. He cautiously navigated the final scramble up a rock slope towards his home. The intricate patchwork of stone and clay formed a cliff dwelling, and a wooden, handmade ladder formed a final defense against any enemy that might assail the tribe, as they lived in their aerie. Pulling the ladder up behind him, he effectively left any approaching enemy with the unenviable task of climbing straight up a sheer cliff to enter the dwelling area. He approached the funny key-shaped door that offered the only entrance to a set of rooms that formed his personal living area. The whole village complex formed an incredible feat of engineering. It was only approachable by following the narrow ledge that yawned over the canyon below. With the ladder pulled up, no human could ever enter the village. It was safe, even from an enemy much more agile than any human. He shivered and fervently hoped it was enough.

~ * ~

I woke with a start and a strange feeling. My head was covered in beads of sweat, and my heart raced. I wasn't sure what happened; I just knew the dream was vivid, and the fear the ancient man felt as he prepared the dwelling for the night was intensely real.

CHAPTER 1

Two Weeks Previously

I couldn't believe it! I was off on an adventure I'd been anticipating for a long time. I had been planning a trip out into Southeastern Utah. I got the time off work and was now driving towards Blanding. My Jeep is perfect for a trip like this, and I was enjoying the drive between Monticello and my destination. This road stretches up into the lower foothills of the Abajo Mountains, and the fields by the highway are always littered with mule deer. It isn't too unusual to see a hundred deer on the short drive between these two small towns.

I idled along with the cruise control set at sixty-five. I didn't feel any need to speed, as the whole area is beautiful, and it's nice to see a cop and not worry about being pulled over. As I drove, I thought a little about my life and where I was going, and where I might end up. I was still young, only thirty-two years old, and I had a good job. I loved my life on the whole and loved the freedom the wide-open spaces of Colorado and Utah gave me.

In a mirror, I would see an average-sized guy, five foot ten, and one hundred eighty pounds. I've always been athletic, and I keep myself in shape by going to the gym and playing racquetball. I have light brown hair, and blue eyes that sometimes have a hint of green in a certain light. I guess I wasn't handsome, but I wasn't ugly either. I'd say I got a pretty good deal of the cards when it came to the physical side of my life.

I felt differently about my social life. While I did have friends, I had been raised by parents who were strict, and used religion as a weapon. They picked and chose the aspects of the Bible they wished to follow. Mostly they considered society in general to be lacking in moral values and as such they severely limited my social interactions, especially with school functions and situations that would allow me to develop social skills. So, I was awkward and shy around people in general and girls in particular.

Even so, life was good, and while I was occasionally frustrated with my social life, I still had hopes for a brighter future.

I pulled into Blanding around three PM. On the phone, I found the Airbnb I had reserved and navigated the small streets of the town, searching for it. I know it might sound strange to want a whole house for just one person, but I enjoy the privacy and the spacious feeling a house provides. Besides, it was my vacation, and I wanted to enjoy myself.

I found the house no problem. The access code worked. I threw my stuff on the couch and headed out to get food. Not a whole lot of options in Blanding, but I was fine with just a burger, and I'd head over to the market for some food for the place—and some last-minute supplies for my hiking trip.

I fueled up at a local joint that offered gas, shopping, bowling, and a fast-food chain, all in one. The food wasn't bad, and I headed down to the market for a few items for the house.

I had most of my supplies for the hiking trip already, so I confined myself to purchases like cereal, milk, and some stuff to drink. And, of course, the fixin's for coffee. I love to make coffee my way.

I headed back to the house and spent a little time packing. It was just an overnight trip, so I didn't need a lot. I made sure my sleeping bag was packed, along with plenty of water. A few packets of food from a sporting goods store, along with some water purification tablets in case of water in the canyon. I also checked for my sunscreen. It can get hot in the canyon, and the sun can really burn if you're not careful. I packed one last item. I put in my 9mm semi- auto. I couldn't imagine needing it, but I like to carry it, just in case.

I woke up in the morning early. I always wake up early. A family curse. I lay in bed for a little while, trying to will myself back to sleep and gave up.

I fixed some coffee, had a bowl of cereal, and surfed the net for a bit. I went ahead and put my gear back into the Jeep. It was time to head out!

I know some people probably wouldn't enjoy a hiking trip by themselves. I can go either way. I really like going out with other people, but I also don't mind an occasional trip on my own. Being on your own is more immediate and refreshing. I find anytime you're with another person you automatically tend to create a little world of your own, whether hiking in a canyon or visiting a foreign country.

Any time you go somewhere on your own, this little shield against the forces that surround you is gone, and it makes you both more vulnerable and more open to new experiences. I guess this can be good or bad, but it's definitely a big difference.

I spent a couple of hours driving and swung off the main road and onto a rugged, single lane dirt lane that hardly deserved the name. I twisted my way through the tree limbs that overhung the seldom used path, navigating my way over ruts, large rocks, and places where one side of the track had washed away.

I was hoping for a way that led to a canyon I had visited with some friends a few years before. We had just been exploring the country, taking different roads and finding out where they went, when a certain road led us to the rim of a magnificent canyon. It was typical Utah landscape; the canyon was steep, with rugged rock- strewn slopes that often ended on the edge of a cliff with a sudden drop of a few hundred feet to the canyon floor. The vista and the grandeur of the place was amazing. Huge red rocks were perched on small pedestals, and even a breath could displace them. The sky was blue and clear, and the piñon and juniper trees interspersed with huge outcroppings of rock created a vivid and striking display. Not only was it beautiful in a stark way, but it also evoked a feeling. The canyon drew me to it. I remember knowing I would be back at some future date.

I continued to make my way towards the canyon. Occasion- ally I would pause at a crossroads, trying to recall which branch of this old road led to the canyon. I would rehash old memories and turn left or right and once again creep nearer to my destination.

A couple of hours later, I reached the rim of the canyon. I parked the Jeep over at the side of the road, mostly surrounded by rocks, except for one small juniper tree. There was no real need to park in a special way, as this was the end of the road, with no sign any other people had even been here in the last few months. I did it anyway. I shouldered my pack, locked the Jeep, and picked my way down the steep slope of the canyon.

The way down was rough but navigable. I'd hate to have to do it in the dark, but that wouldn't be an issue, as I was planning on sleeping in the bottom. It would be a little scary, spending a night out in the middle of the wilderness with no other human beings for miles around, but it would also be memorable.

I continued down, and as I approached the bottom, I found myself in a small wash. I followed it towards the canyon floor, and as I continued on, the wash grew steeper. I found myself treading between two rock walls.

The wash grew narrower as it approached the main stream-bed, and I was between two walls higher than my head. The walls tightened even more. I could reach out and touch them on either side of me as I broke out of the wash and into the main portion of the canyon.

At mid-afternoon, I stopped for a few moments to rest. I found a couple of rocks nearby that could serve as a chair and table. The best part was they were also in the shade. I took out one of my water bottles and finished half of it. I had a granola bar and an apple. It was enough for now, and I wanted to find a comfortable place to bed down for the night.

I chose to go down the creek rather than up. After all, it's always easier to go downhill, right? I eased around a gentle bend in the canyon, navigating around various rocks and small trees that were in the way. The creek spilled down a dry waterfall, and I had to find a way around the steep drop off, as it was about ten feet from the top of the large boulder to the floor below. A deep pool of water nestled in the cavity below, and I shivered as I peered down at it. I can't swim, and I had a flash of unease as I thought about what would have happened if I had slipped off the rock and into the pool. I went ahead and skirted the drop-off into the pool, finding a narrow trail that led around the body of water, and I continued on in the dry streambed.

The canyon narrowed and deepened for a couple hundred yards, hindering my view. The walls of the gorge dropped away, propelling me out into a large open area. The creek split, and a sage brush infested mesa like area rose in the middle of the canyon. It was about twenty feet above the creek, and I had to clamber a bit as I struggled up the steep area that abutted the small streambed. I broke out over the top. The tabletop of land was about one hundred yards wide, and it extended down the canyon a quarter of a mile. The mesa was composed of a large area of brush on the upper end, where I stood, and it transmuted into an area of juniper and piñon trees towards the other end.

Some small pot shards were scattered around the open areas of sage brush. No doubt the Anasazi used this as a farming area. One painted piece caught my eye and I knelt to examine it more closely. The brilliant geometric patterns, black on white, made for a fantastically beautiful piece, and I took out my phone and snapped a picture of it.

I spent the remainder of the afternoon exploring the mesa. It was a beautiful area, large and open, yet surrounded by the rugged red and white variegated cliffs that the Utah area is famous for. The brushy area was really flat, but the treed area was slightly more rugged, with a small hilly area just before the mesa started to narrow down. I climbed to the top of the last hill and stared down at an interesting area at the end of the land mass. The hill sloped gently down to a space that was mostly devoid of vegetation.

The mesa started to fade away here, so it was only about a hundred feet wide, and the uplift was flat once again. The few morsels of brush that grew in this area were small, only about eighteen inches tall, and widely interspersed with a smooth rocky area. The rocks were smooth here though, rather than the usual sharp-edged ones that littered the rest of the canyon. I also noticed the stones were all dark in color, a light black. Maybe a geological aberration, I thought. The rocks had been burnt slightly, maybe by some type of volcanic action.

The sun dipped near the edge of the canyon rim. It would be getting dark soon, so I climbed back up the hill and headed toward the main part of the mesa. I searched for a good place to make camp and found a nice opening in the trees at the top of the small hilly area. I would have a good view of the whole canyon from here. I planned on watching the sun set and return on the other side of the canyon in the morning.

I laid out my small air mattress and smoothed out my sleeping bag on top of it. I had a small, one-burner camp stove, and I heated up a can of stew to enjoy with the setting of the sun.

The sky turned a magnificent purple-like color as the darkness set in around me. The temperature rapidly grew cooler, as it often does in the high desert. *I might as well turn in. No smart phones here, no books, no TV. Of course, I could watch a video I had on my phone.* But it seemed somehow "wrong" to do that in this area, so devoid of any sign of the world in which I lived. So, I settled into the bag, wriggling a bit as I tried to find a comfortable position for sleeping. I found my "spot," sighed softly, and drifted off.

Suddenly I was jarred from sleep. I felt confusion, as the sleep fogged my brain. Where was I? I felt for the light I kept on the nightstand in my apartment. I searched for the digital clock I keep as well. I like to know what time it is when I wake up in the middle of the night.

Slowly my brain cleared, and I remembered where I was. There was no nightstand, just a large flat rock. I relaxed for a moment, trying to figure out what woke me. I knew something had interrupted my slumber.

I heard it. Coyotes were howling down the canyon. It's an eerie sound when you're all alone, in the dark, miles from civilization. Yet it was also beautiful, in a way, and I curled up in the sleeping bag, listening to the haunting music of their cries.

Something changed. I didn't pick up on it at first, but I slowly noticed a strange rhythm to the howling. Normally one coyote will start to howl, and others will join in. They'll continue for a bit and slowly trail off into silence. But this was different. I noticed a very measured cadence to their cries. This wasn't just the sounds of animals doing their thing. This was planned out. It was almost music, as if they were performing a piece by a famous composer. Ludwig Van Coyotehoven, I found myself thinking, ridiculously. Perhaps not.

I continued to listen, entranced by it all. Their howls became more structured, as if they were finding their groove. A few howls would begin the song, very soft and low, and they would slowly add voices to the composition, ending in a crashing crescendo. The crazy thing is that a definite sense of timing went on. Da da-da-da, da-da-da, da-da-da...DA-DA... Up and down they went, their refrain bearing a bizarre resemblance to *Figaro*. I couldn't stand it anymore. I got up, dressed, and put on my pack. I was insanely curious to get closer to these animals and to maybe see them. After all, the full moon was out, and enough light for me to move around as long as I was careful.

I moved towards the sound, picking my way down the slope of the hill. The light of the moon cast cold shadows around me. The rim of the canyon towered above me in the distance, and the whole canyon was resplendent in the soft illumination. Glittering with darkness, the stark beauty around me was incredible.

I made my way around a small patch of trees, the sound of the coyotes drawing me ever onwards. I stepped into a small ravine, and I remembered the unusual clearing of black rocks that formed the end of the mesa-like uplift I was on. I knew that's where they had to be, the open area a perfect place for a gathering. I clambered up towards the final barrier between the ravine and the clearing. A few trees right at the crest of the hill formed a natural border for the clearing. While I climbed, I noticed a flickering light: yellow and orange, inhabiting the top branches. It had to be coming from the clearing. What was it?

I slowed my pace instinctively, not wanting to make any noise even though the coyotes were busy creating their music. I was excited by the thought of what was happening in the clearing, but in the back of my mind, the lizard brain, so to speak, I felt a sudden rush of panic. Something was telling me to run, to retreat. Ancient memories were bubbling to the surface. I stopped, indecisive. I wanted to see what was in the clearing, but I also didn't want to see. I stood, pondering, but I thought to myself, "If you leave now, you'll be kicking yourself for the rest of your life. You'll always wonder what was happening with the coyotes, and you'll regret not looking."

So, my front brain took charge of my hindbrain, and I eased up the slope, drawing nearer to the small copse of juniper and piñon in front of me. I used the trunks and low hanging branches to shield myself, and I worked my way through a small thicket of young trees. I carefully eased my head over the small juniper and peered out into the clearing.

The scene in front was bizarre and unbelievable. A large bonfire brightened the middle of the open area. Three smaller blazes were burning at the edges of the space, lighting the whole expanse in a lurid glare of burning embers. Coyotes were everywhere. Some were on all fours, but others not. Some walked upright on their hind legs. Many howled, adding their voices to the orchestra. Others just stood, both on two and four legs, appearing to enjoy the festivities. Still others danced around the large fire in the center of the glade. They danced on two legs only, and they whirled and swayed, all in unison, like waves passing through a wheat field, driven by the wind.

I gazed out across the clearing, numb with shock. I was having a hard time believing what I was seeing. I just stared for a few minutes, taking it all in, trying to grasp what I saw, attempting to accept the fact that in front of me things were happening that were "impossible".

One coyote caught my eye. He was standing upright on a large white rock. He stood to the left of the large blaze in the center, just outside the dancers. He was larger than the others, much larger. He was the same height as an adult human, close to six feet tall. I couldn't tell for sure because of the distance and smoke in the air, but he was wearing a hat. Also, he wore a jacket.

I watched as he swayed to the music. He seemed to be of the other coyotes, but also not of them. I was hypnotized. How could a coyote be this large? And was he really wearing clothing?

Then it happened. I stared at him too long. He suddenly cocked his head and swung around, locking his gaze upon me. I ducked back into the shelter of the tree branches as he did so, suddenly shivering with fear. I wasn't sure if he actually saw me or not, and so I risked taking another gander at the clearing. I changed positions slightly and poked my head out above the branches of a tree. The ritual in front of me continued, but Coyote, and the rock on which he stood, were both gone.

I knew I needed to get out and get out now. Whatever it was I had just witnessed, I was sure the coyotes didn't want us humans to know about it. I was also sure they'd gladly kill to make sure it stayed a secret.

I crept up the canyon. It was still dark out, and the craggy bluffs above stood out starkly against the mostly full moon that shone in the sky. I drew in a couple of breaths, trying to quell my fear and breathe less noisily. I couldn't afford to let them find me. I slowly picked my way carefully across the rocky ground. It would be very easy to turn an ankle if I slipped off a rock or stepped in a prairie dog hole. Either way, I'd be finished.

There up ahead. Was that the trail up? I couldn't remember, and it was so hard to tell. Everything looks different in the dark. It was just a fractured jumble of darkness, interspersed with fragments of lighter patches where the moon shone through the trees.

Sometimes trees look like monsters. Have you ever noticed

how cottonwoods, when denuded of leaves, have eerie, even sinister shapes? They loom over you, with their twisted, misshapen branches branding the sky with an agony of regret and sorrow.

I breathed faster now, my heart raced, as I wrestled with my panic. "I've got to keep it under control," I told myself. "As long as I don't lose it here, I'll be all right." And I began to succeed. I felt my fear lessen a bit, and my thoughts became more logical, less scattered.

I continued inching up the gorge, and the walls narrowed. On the right side the trees fell away, a high, implacable wall of rock replacing the wiry branches. Up ahead was a break in the canyon wall, a wisp of moonlight shining through the opening, creating a luminous shaft that shattered the darkness on both sides, a sign, pointing the way out.

I entered a narrow passage formed in the sandstone bluff of the right side of the canyon and labored up a steep slope. The passage opened into an area of small trees interspersed with rocks. Some of the rocks were taller than I am, and the shadows they cast created pockets of implacable blackness surrounded by pale moonlight. A stark beauty resides in this.

I inched up the steep slope to a small bench to rest. I chose the right way to continue. A big bunch of trees stood to the left, a brooding mass of unknown quantity. To the right a ledge of rock jutted out. It stood about six feet high, perfectly vertical, enough to thwart his efforts, but still better than the trees. I approached it, and spotted a couple of small handholds, resting in pools of inky darkness that resisted my best efforts to pierce them.

Could a snake be in there? Who knows, maybe a cactus or some other type of danger?

Regardless, it was better than trying to navigate through the trees and I gingerly stuck my right hand into the first handhold. I held my breath and cringed as I slowly explored the small crevice, expecting to encounter a set of fangs or the needles of a prickly pear at any moment. Neither happened though, and I found a handhold. I firmly gripped it, levered myself up, and repeated the process with my left hand at the next handhold. I cleared that as well, and slowly clambered to the top of the ledge.

I made it past the worst of it now, and the canyon rim stood before me, up a gentle slope littered with small rocks and vegetation. I breathed easier for the remaining distance to the canyon rim and felt hope and optimism suffuse my being. The end of my journey was near. I was jubilant as I closed the last hundred feet, the thought I may actually make it, that I was going to escape, propelling me forward.

I clambered over the rim of the canyon; the rock ledge a mere foot high, just a shadow of the ones that I traversed below. *It's as if everything is suddenly going my way.*

My car was parked just over a rise, and I headed toward it, picking up my pace as I went, the nearness to safety lending strength to my legs, which were shaking with exhaustion. I was eager to get away from this whole experience, to leave it behind me.

And voila! I was able to make out the shape of the car, a juxtaposition of regular rectangles jutting out of the soft irregular shapes of bushes and rocks that surrounded it.

I neared the vehicle, and...

A light flared; that of a match. I caught a brief glimpse of gray hair and whiskers, the soft glint of a pipe. *Damn, it's him. Who knows why Coyote has such a fixation on things English, but he does.* From the bowler hat perched jauntily on his canine head, to the exaggerated hump on his ivory bowl pipe, to the red blazer, he exuded a sartorial elegance. Also, a bit of conceit, as he casually waited, making it plain the escape effort was just part of the game, as if my efforts to get away were always too little, too late.

The fox hunting outfit he chose for this exchange is no accident, that's for sure.

My stomach clenched with fear and confusion. How could he possibly be waiting for me? My mind fluttered with indecision, and I felt a chill run through me, the same way an impala must feel when being stalked by a lion. I was literally frozen to the ground, rooted to the spot, consumed with dread.

I silently watched as Coyote slowly drew through the pipe, casually blowing a pall of smoke into the air.

Coyote seemed to be unaware of my presence, casually puffing on his pipe as if he were enjoying an early morning smoke before calling the hounds to go on a hunt.

I knew better, though. He was just toying with me. Making me feel the way a mouse must feel when a cat has him and plays with him, feeding on his terror as if it is a dessert, maybe a crème brûlée or an ice cream sundae.

I remembered I had the pistol in my pack. I had carefully put it in the side pocket for easy access in case I encountered a rattlesnake. Maybe this wasn't over after all.

Casually, breathlessly, I inched my left hand back until my fumbling fingers encountered the pack. Coyote was still enjoying his smoke, no doubt relishing the feeling of despair his presence created.

I felt around and found the flap. I struggled with the snap, and it opened, creating an almost inaudible "snick" as it did so.

Coyote stiffened and paused, his pipe comically hovering a few inches from his long muzzle.

I found the grip of the pistol. I silently oriented my hand around the firearm and pulled it from the pack. Quickly, praying I'd be able to do it in time, I grabbed the action and worked it, racking a bullet into the chamber from the magazine.

I raised the pistol, aiming at my vehicle, right where Coyote was standing. I couldn't make him out. God damn it, where did he go. I strained my eyes, feverishly searching for any sign of movement. The moonlight was bright, which helped, but the darkness of the shadows still covered areas where Coyote could be, ready to pounce.

I waited for a few seconds, searching the area in front. A juniper sat to the right of the Jeep. It was about ten feet tall, not very large at all, but the shadow it cast almost reached the car, the most likely place for Coyote to be. I didn't see anything, and I tried using the corner of my eye. It was easier to catch a slight movement that way, as if the eye was more attuned to a life of hunting, slaying, or even escaping, and evading when used in that fashion.

I crept towards the Jeep, keeping one eye out for any type of motion, and cursed to myself. The key to the car was in my pocket. It was remote, of course, but I still needed to dig it out of my pocket to activate the lock. I shifted the gun to my right hand, my off hand, and dug into my left pocket.

I felt for the keys and snagged them between my thumb and forefinger. Slowly I drew them out. I felt for the buttons, trying to figure out which one was for opening the door. Usually, I knew which one was which, but I felt panic fogging my mind, and I just couldn't remember which button was the right one. I decided on the upper one and pushed the small square of plastic with my thumb.

Instantly a siren blared, filling the night with a blasting noise to wake the dead. I jumped; I'd hit the panic button.

A part of the shadow from the juniper tree materialized into a canine form! I guess the panic button scared Coyote as well. I instinctively pointed the pistol at the dark form bolting towards me. I fired, once, twice, and then emptied the whole magazine into the darkness. I waited for a few seconds hunched over, breathing hard. Nothing happened, no movement. I mentally took hold of my emotions, forcing down the raw panic and felt the key fob once again.

I found the same button I'd pushed before and managed to shut off the alarm. I found the right button, and the welcoming rumble of opening locks met my ears. I jumped into the jeep, locked the doors, and started the engine. I turned on the lights. Shifting into reverse, I swung the vehicle to the left and watched as the headlights illuminated the area where Coyote had rushed me only moments before.

I was flabbergasted. I had fully expected to see the form of a dead animal stretched out on the ground. I hesitated, afraid to get out of the protective shield of the car, but I just had to know. I opened the door and gingerly stepped out. I made my way to the spot where Coyote should have been, the former darkness now a bright halo of white. On the uneven ground in front, the brown earth interspersed with small tufts of grass and small rocks. Nothing. There was no sign of blood, and even stranger, I couldn't make out any tracks. It didn't make sense, not that any of this made sense, I mean since when did coyotes use fire, and have strange rituals down in canyons?

The feeling of being exposed overcame my curiosity. I hopped into the Jeep and headed back towards civilization; glad I was going to put this whole camping trip behind me. I'd even be glad to go back to work.

CHAPTER 2

Audrey hiked along the trail. She was second in line, following her dad. Her kid brother came next, and her mom brought up the rear. This way her mother could make sure both kids (mostly her little brother) were safe and keeping up. Also, her younger sibling Tim had the tendency to see what interested him and dart to the side to check out a funny tree or a rabbit or a lizard.

Audrey was twelve years old but very precocious for her age. She loved going on these hikes out in the back country in Utah. Sure, it meant several hours away from social media, because cell phone reception was usually nonexistent, but it was easy enough to catch up with her circle when she got back in range. Also, she usually had some cool pictures to post of her hikes. She liked having different items to share with her friends.

Audrey was a typical girl in many ways. In other ways she was not. She was still a few years shy of her full height, but she was already five feet, only lacking an inch or two, and she was very fit. She not only hiked but also enjoyed all types of athletic activities. She had been practicing jujitsu since she was seven and really loved going to her classes. She found the combination of physical and mental conditioning gave a big boost to her self-confidence, at a time in her life when this was very helpful. She was lightly freckled, with auburn hair and green eyes. This somehow made her name, Audrey, perfect.

It was a beautiful day for a hike. The sky was the deep blue that comes with an atmosphere that is virtually free of smog or any other contaminants. The red earth and green trees contrasted beautifully with the sky, a vibrant, brilliant aroma of warm colors woven together to create the beginning of a magnificent morning. It was a little warm out but not hot. It was easy enough for the family to cool down by stopping under the welcoming shade of a tree for a few moments.

They were heading for a canyon on a little used trail. The trail head was about one-and-one-half miles from the rim of the gorge, and they were strolling casually, conserving their energy for the more demanding descent down a steep slope, and, of course, the return trip back up planned for later in the afternoon. Audrey's dad topped out on a small rise and paused, allowing the rest of them to catch up. The four of them stood gazing at the scenery in front of them. The trail was visible as it wound through the trees, rising slightly as it neared the canyon rim. It was as if the canyon had been gouged out of the earth by a huge plow, and both sides of the canyon were higher than the surrounding countryside, the remnants of the original furrow piled millions of years ago.

They stood for a few minutes more, not speaking, their easy familiarity making words unnecessary. Her dad adjusted his pack slightly, readying himself to continue, when her brother pointed towards the distant canyon rim and asked.

"What's that?"

"Where, what do you see?" all three of them asked in unison.

He pointed again. "Right there!"

Then they all saw it. The landscape near the canyon was changing. The trees and the earth were twisting and contorting in bizarre, unnatural paroxysms of pain. It seemed as if the earth was fighting a losing battle, and some power was altering portions of the land in front of them. The trees and dirt would start frantically writhing in a strange parody of dance and suddenly become motionless. The affected area appeared different than it did before. The phenomenon was still too far away to make out details, but it was obvious the land was somehow transformed. The new area was dead. The trees still existed, but only as lifeless husks, their bare branches a testament to the power that had transformed them. The earth itself had a dull gray appearance.

"I wonder what that is?" Audrey's father asked.

"I'm not sure what it is," her mother replied. "But I think it might be dangerous. Maybe it's an earthquake. Let's head back to the car, just in case."

Her dad hesitated, both alarmed and curious. However, common sense and the concern for his family took hold, and he nodded.

"Yeah, let's go back, just to be on the safe side."

"Let's check it out before we go," Tim offered, irrepressible as always

"No," her mother replied firmly. "We don't know what it is or what's causing it. It could be dangerous. Let's go," she said, allowing a bit of steel to enter her voice, just enough to let Tim know she was serious.

Tim knew when he was beat and turned around. They headed back towards the car, about three quarters of a mile away. Now they marched in the opposite formation, Audrey's mom leading and her dad bringing up the rear.

They continued for several minutes in this fashion, all of them occasionally casting a curious gaze over their shoulders. They didn't see anything, the small rise they had rested on cutting off their sight towards the canyon rim.

Then they froze, a fierce byproduct of shock and fear. Audrey's mother made a small, sharp intake of breath, and Tim shrank against his parents.

Only a hundred yards in front of them, the same strange anomaly was affecting the land between them and their car. It was much closer this time, and they watched for a few moments, transfixed by the spectacle. The transformation was eerily silent. They heard no sound at all, which was incongruous considering a piñon tree suddenly shivered, and it jerkily wrenched its branches. It swayed and trembled, branches moving spasmodically, as if it were being electrocuted. The tree strained, and the stress it was undergoing was palpable. It heaved, and all at once the entire tree whipped to the right, as if assailed a hurricane force wind, its limbs stretched out and the tree bent itself at a terrific angle to the ground. After a pause, the tree froze in this state, and it became an old gray trunk, that appeared to have been devoid of leaves for many years.

The ground was enduring a similar battle. The soil itself was rising and falling in painful convulsions. At the same time the tree was transformed, the landscape under it changed as well. The topsoil was buckling; shattered shards of material rising up in the air, twisting as it rose. Then it would hesitate, defying gravity for a few moments, before plunging back to its original resting place. The earth would tremble for a moment and eventually subside. The soil turned a dull gray, fading to black in places. Dull and lifeless as an airless planetoid, it defied any form of life to encroach upon it and survive.

Audrey felt her panic building and instinctively moved closer to her dad. He responded by putting his arm around her shoulders and drawing her close. Tim and her mom drew close with them, and briefly they stood, just like that, clinging to one another.

"Let's try to go around it," her dad said. "If that doesn't work, we'll try to go through it. I'm not sure what it is, but it might not be dangerous."

He strode off, breaking from the trail, at an angle designed to skirt the outer border of the phenomenon. Audrey and Tim followed closely, and her mom stayed right behind them. Her dad quickened his pace slightly, anxious to get around the spectacle and back to the safety of the car. They neared the abnormal landscape. They could see the changes the earth was suffering, and instinctively drew back from it.

Her father veered to the right when they got about fifty feet from the anomaly, and they walked parallel to it. He had increased his pace again, his speed revealing his increasing anxiety about the strange phenomenon blocking their path.

A coyote appeared in front of them. It was probably confused and frightened by what was happening, just like they were. It didn't appear to be afraid of them at all. It just stood directly in their path, watching them. Her dad hesitated, not wanting a confrontation with the animal. He deliberated, not wishing to get any closer to the aberration, but also not interested in taking a detour that would take them farther from the car.

He decided to risk getting closer to the strange landscape, and so veered slightly left, intending to skirt around the coyote. As he turned slightly, drawing the family closer to the twisting trees, another coyote appeared, again directly in front of them. He glanced to the right at the other coyote. Now with no other choice, they were going to have to confront one of the animals. Her dad was cautious but not overly concerned. After all, a coyote wasn't that large of an animal, only weighing about forty-five pounds. He considered picking up a rock or large stick, but decided that might come off as confrontational, so instead headed slowly toward the coyote directly in front of him. He hoped the natural fear instinct would kick in as he drew closer and the beast would retreat, leaving an open space for his small group to move by.

The coyotes didn't move as he drew closer, so he hesitated and yelled at the animals, waving his arms, thinking this might startle them, causing them to bolt. They didn't move or respond to his yells, instead just gazed at him, as impassive and coldly logical as a Vulcan. He once again hesitated, unsure of himself. He could see the end of the aberration in front of him. It was only a hundred feet or so where the border of the event was taking place. It was very narrow here, at its end, just a long finger extending out from a broader swath of misshapen land behind them. All the family needed was a clear path, and they would be free.

He moved forward a few more steps and slowed. Another coyote appeared, and then another. The four of them presented an increasingly difficult obstacle between the family and the edge of the barrier. Her father stopped, and the rest of the family was brought up hard behind him. They stared at the coyotes, trying to fathom their intent. Were they running from the aberration as well, or did they have other motives. The coyotes stared silently back at him, a living, breathing impediment to the freedom that lay just minutes beyond.

He stopped, and a wave of dread washed over him. He got the feeling the coyotes weren't present because of the transformations in the terrain. Or rather, it wasn't due to panic or confusion. Maybe they were in collusion with the transformation, a part of it, somehow. He spied a rock about the size of his fist and picked it up. He hefted before flinging it at the coyotes, not meaning to hit them. He just wanted to scare them a little. Perhaps this would break them up, allowing the family an opportunity to break for the open ground that lay so close, so inviting, like a branch that lies just out of reach of a drowning man.

The first rock landed near two of the coyotes, but they didn't respond to it at all. They glanced at it indifferently and returned their gaze to the family in front of them. He picked up another rock, and in a moment of anger and desperation, threw it as hard as he could at the coyote directly in front of him. The rock flew true, speeding towards the coyote, and he found himself willing the rock to hit it, to hurt it. He didn't care about the coyote anymore; he just wanted to break free of them.

He watched hopefully as the rock neared the coyote, and disappointment welled up in him as the animal neatly stepped to one side, like a ballet dancer gracefully performing a move, and the stone sailed past, hitting the ground with a dull, futile thud.

He grabbed another rock and threw it and another. Both times the coyotes adroitly dodged the projectiles. He picked up a large branch that had broken off a tree, and brandishing it, rushed the coyotes, hoping they would scatter.

The coyotes didn't scatter. Instead, they split up into groups of two. Smoothly they separated, like water in a stream split in two by a large rock. As he continued to approach, one coyote on each side of him circled behind him, out of sight. They were prepared to attack him from his blind side.

Audrey's mom screamed at them, "Get out of here. Leave us alone! All we want is to leave."

Then she pleaded with her husband, "Brandon, come back. I'm afraid they're going to attack if you go any farther."

Brandon considered and retreated, returning to his family.

Two more coyotes appeared, forming a rough semi-circle in front of them. Two more appeared, adding their number to the crowd. Suddenly one of them stood up on his hind legs briefly and uttered a sharp, barking sound. A couple of the others repeated the process. Two more appeared.

At this point it was apparent they were in terrible danger. Audrey felt panic rising in her, but she summoned her martial arts training to find her center. She used some breathing exercises, and as she felt herself begin to calm down, she considered her options. She faced the twisting landscape that hovered just fifty feet away. "Mom, Dad," she cried. "Let's go over to the edge of that thing. Maybe the coyotes will be afraid to follow us."

Her mom and dad exchanged quick glances and nodded. All four broke into a quick trot, arriving at the edge of the phenomenon shortly. Her dad hesitated and gingerly stuck his hand out towards the edge of the altered terrain. His hand broached the border, and he gasped in pain, quickly retracting his exposed digits.

"It felt like I was getting cut by razor blades," he gasped, glaring at his hand. They all studied his fingers but found no apparent damage.

"I don't see anything," Audrey's mom said. "Let me try."

She slowly extended her hand toward the border, touched the edge and inched past it. Instantly she gasped and swiftly pulled her hand back. "You're right," she said. "It's like I'm being cut to pieces."

"I'm scared, Mommy." Timmy began crying.

Audrey noticed a branch a few feet away. It wasn't large; she knew Timmy could manage it. She grabbed it and swiftly returned to her younger brother.

"Here," she said with all the confidence she could muster. "You take this. If they get close, you whack 'em good."

Tim grabbed the branch and his cries subsided, momentarily mollified by the weapon in his hand.

Audrey could see the other side of the anomaly beside her; it was only about thirty feet wide here. Maybe if she took off running, she could make it through to the normal ground that lay beyond. Another thought hit her. At the very least, people needed to know what was happening out here. She fished her cell phone out of her pack and entered a text message as a draft. There was no reception, of course, but the draft would be saved.

She entered the following: "Hello, my name is Audrey Butler. I'm out here hiking with my mom, dad, and brother. Something really weird is going on. The trees and ground are changing, and a bunch of coyotes have us trapped."

She quickly entered settings and disabled the password protection so anyone could open the phone. She took her phone in her hand, and, using all her force, she flung it toward the normal ground that lay not far across the twisted landscape. The cell phone flashed in the sun, lazily turning on its own axis, as it described a perfect arc through the air. She felt triumph as she saw it land well beyond the border of the phenomenon, safely in the normal terrain that lay beyond. She heard her mother scream and turned.

Even more coyotes now, over a dozen closed in on the family uttering short barks and howls. Occasionally one of them would jump up on its hind legs for a few seconds. Her mother and father both had thick branches, and her brother had the smaller one she had found. She could see the desperation and fear on her parents' faces. They were terrified, not only of the situation, but by the fact they may not be able to protect their children.

She foraged for a branch or weapon, preparing to join the rest of her family. What she saw took the heart out of her.

Another coyote appeared, rambling casually through the trees and out into the small opening in front. He was much larger than the others and held himself on his hind legs as easily as a human would. He had the normal markings in his fur, but in other ways he was very different from the animals surrounding them. His front legs were shaped much like a typical canine, but they joined his body at his shoulders in a way that was closer to the way a human's arms are joined to a torso, giving him the ability move and use tools in a man-like fashion. His paws, longer than a normal animal's, ended in claws. The soft pads underneath were elongated, and his fifth finger was formed much as a thumb, giving him an opposable digit.

He was dressed in a red blazer, and he had a black bowler hat on his head. His eyes shone with a ferocious intelligence. He strode up confidently to the front line of coyotes and stopped. He looked at the family briefly, but he appeared preoccupied with another matter. He lifted his hand-paws out in front of him, hummed a low chant to himself, and dropped them to his sides.

Audrey knew the change affecting the landscape around them had stopped. She also understood the change was somehow caused by this creature in front of her. She had a sudden idea. If the change had stopped, maybe it was possible to pass over the misshapen terrain now. She slipped back, and quickly stuck her hand across the edge of the altered ground. Immediately a pain like a series of small razor blades attacked her fingers and hands. She gasped and withdrew her hand.

She turned back. The coyotes advanced. Their yipping and howling increased in volume and frequency, like an opera reaching its crescendo, and the sound echoed in the air. Her mother suddenly appeared before her. She stared at Audrey intensely for a moment and spoke.

"Audrey, you're the bravest, most spirited girl I have ever known. I love you more than life itself. I know in my heart that if any of us has a chance to survive this, it's going to be you. Now, I want you to run into whatever this is in front of us. I don't care how much it hurts. I want you to make it to the other side. Do you understand?"

Audrey nodded her head, unable to speak, as she felt tears well up in her eyes.

"Good, now turn around," her mother said fiercely. "Now move a couple of steps closer."

Audrey moved until she brushed the border of the aberration.

"Are you ready?" her mother asked.

Audrey breathed out, and answered, "Yes Mom, I'm ready."

"Good," her mother said, and shoved Audrey as hard as she could, launching her into the phenomenon. "Now run," she screamed. "Run. RUN. RUN!"

Audrey ran. Her mother's shove and her words propelling her deeper into the twisted space. Thousands of invisible razors slashed every part of her body. Her eyes, legs, stomach, all felt as if they were being sliced open. She ran, trying to will her body across the perverted area to the normal ground that lay not far beyond. She reached the midpoint and stumbled. She staggered a couple more steps and stumbled again. She slowed and came to a shambling halt. Her body sagged toward the earth. She made another try to get back to her feet, but the pain from the invisible razors was too great. She felt as if the razors were not only cutting into her flesh but also her spirit, as if the effect was more spiritual than physical.

I'm not gonna make it, she thought, just before she lost consciousness and fell to the ground, still well within the borders of the aberration.

CHAPTER 3

Coyote lowered his arms. The "wrinkle," as he called it, was large enough to trap the four humans in front of him. Creating this physical aberration of the land required tremendous concentration and was very taxing, so he was glad to be finished with it.

He watched the humans, desperately flopping and gasping, searching in vain for some hole in the net he'd cast, and mused once again how similar this was to a fox hunt. He was tremendously knowledgeable about happenings in all corners of the world, and he remembered how, upon hearing about the English and the hunt, he was delighted and obsessed with the ritual. He remembered learning that many justified the sport by citing the need for "pest control." Humans certainly met the criteria for pests, just like foxes, maybe even more so. After all, didn't they spread and consume all the game in an area? As the fox might deplete all the resources at a certain chicken house, didn't humans deplete all the resources of the entire planet? He found humans and their outrage at a simple beast merely doing what nature had equipped it to do, while ignoring their own depredations, fascinating.

He remembered how he decided he had to have a blazer and a hat. It fit his sense of humor and outlook on life. So, he had begun, slowly singing, weaving his spell, in a low rumbling voice. He sang for three nights, slowly shaping and coaxing, and when he was ready, he reached out and gently folded the earth.

It was rather simple for him to step through, into the empty department store known as "Harrods." He still remembered the feeling of childlike awe as he roamed the aisles of the store, gazing at all the different items on display. He enjoyed the clicking of his claws on the slick marble floors. He chose a nice red blazer. He picked a black bowler hunting hat. It went with the blazer rather well, he thought. Those were the only two items he had originally wanted, but in the various displays, he spied a magnificent ivory pipe. It was intricately carved, and he loved the elegant deep curve of its stem as it molded itself to the bowl, so he picked it up as well. After his brief "shopping spree" he stepped back through and released his hold upon the earth, letting it return to its usual form.

As for humans, did anyone feel anything when Coyote folded the earth? Perhaps a few moaned in their sleep, their dreams full of shifting sands, or a sudden feeling they were falling out of bed. As for those awake, probably some sensitive souls felt a slight quiver in their stomach. Perhaps some briefly found themselves thinking "EARTHQUAKE," but by and large this event passed by the annals of history, completely unnoticed and unremarked upon.

Coyote had this "shopping trip" over a century ago, as humans count time, but he had no difficulty keeping his blazer and hat tidy.

Whenever he noticed either item was starting to show any sign of age or wear, he would take it in his paw like hands and sing to it. He would sing a different song than he used for folding the earth, for each ritual required its own song. But the song to repair a physical item was short, and he could return his attire to "off the shelf new" in less than an hour.

The change he had wrought in the earth in order to capture the family was different. It required constant upkeep, and he had started it earlier in the day. He sang a great roaring song to begin the process, but once it started, he maintained and controlled it by humming. As he climbed from the canyon, he hummed, and shaped the phenomenon to carefully block any chance of escape by the family in front of him. He was able to communicate with his lesser brethren, the animals humans thought of as coyotes, to a certain extent. He used them to keep an eye on the family until he arrived at the scene. When it was enough, he stopped humming, allowing the transformation to freeze in place.

He watched with mild amusement as the humans rushed about, this way and that, overrun with fear and uncertainty. Now he watched as the female who must be the mother knelt by her young one, the girl. They exchanged a few words, and a brief hug, probably some type of farewell ritual, Coyote mused. They both approached the edge of the twisted region, the wrinkle he had created.

Now this was getting good; he watched with avid curiosity,

waiting to see what they would do. The young one approached the wrinkle, stopping just at its edge. Out of nowhere, the mother gave her a great shove, into it. To Coyote's astonishment the young girl didn't scream or turn back or try to escape the pain she was obviously enduring. Instead, she ran directly into the middle of the wrinkle. He watched, incredulous. Of all the hunts he had led, over the countless years of his existence on this earth, very few had ever willingly braved the pain the wrinkle inflicted.

He watched her head into the middle, both irritated at her escape and grandly curious as to whether she would make it to the other side. He even found himself rooting for her, just a little bit. She wasn't going to make it. She slowed and fell.

His creation had successfully captured her.

The mother grabbed her young cub, the little boy, and was talking intently to him. Coyote immediately understood she was trying to save her young.

Allowing one young cub to escape was lamentable, but allowing two to escape would be disastrous. It was already embarrassing enough, and he had his reputation to think about.

He relaxed and concentrated, sending a signal to the coyotes that surrounded him. The coyotes understood and massed, bracing themselves to attack.

Now coyotes have a cruel, malicious streak to their nature at any time. They will find a dog in a yard, especially out in the country, and start howling at it. As the howling continues the dog will become more and more agitated, howling with the coyotes. If no humans remain to talk to him, and he can find a way out of the yard, he will dart out to join his canine brothers. They will, of course, kill any dog unfortunate enough to make it out to "join" the pack.

When Coyote is present, he emanates a power that gives the lesser animals strength, courage, and a will for depredation.

So, when Coyote released the animals, they didn't hesitate.

They fell upon the humans.

Meanwhile Coyote approached the barrier. He was interested in the young girl. He knew from experience; that although he was the creator of the wrinkle, he was still vulnerable to it. He tentatively reached out, his paw-hand a few centimeters from the edge of the anomaly. He briefly tested the barrier, flinched, and hurriedly withdrew his paw-hand as the expected razor-like pain needled into it. He hunched his head forward slightly and sniffed. He couldn't smell anything at least not of the girl. The barrier blocked him. A bit nostalgic, he remembered a young Pueblo girl he had caught once, for some reason out at night, by herself. The marrow of her bones had been particularly sweet if he recalled correctly.

He silenced the pang of regret in his stomach. A pragmatic sort by nature, he abandoned that which was out of his reach and turned, not wanting to miss the feast taking place behind him.

An hour later it was finished. Coyote smacked his lips and belched. He watched as the coyotes squabbled over the bones. That was all that was left now. Two of his brethren were busy tugging at some ribs, one on one end, and one on the other. They continued tugging, and slowly the ribs gave way with a wet cracking sound. Both of the coyotes landed on their rears and triumphantly headed for the canyon, each carrying their prize with them. All that was left of the family was a circle of bloody dirt. He knew it was unacceptable. He relaxed, found his center, and hummed.

Soon his humming grew louder and was occasionally sprinkled with words. The words were ancient, guttural, and strewn with multi syllabic jumbles of consonants, with very few vowels. No person on earth would understand the language, because it was his primal vernacular, much older than any language known to man. A philologist would have been surprised, however, to recognize a few of the words as similar to words in use by different Southern Athabaskan tribes. A native speaker of Navajo or Apache would find a few of the words understandable, although they wouldn't recognize enough of the vocabulary to get a gist of what Coyote was saying.

Coyote continued his ritual, humming and singing, coaxing the sullied land in front of him to his will. He continued, and the soil in front of him cleansed itself, the dirt returning to just dirt, the stones oozing blood into thin air. He continued in this vein for over an hour, and at the end, the landscape had returned to its original appearance, as if nothing had happened.

Coyote glanced at the altered landscape beside him. He could see the edges already starting to recede. He knew from experience the manifestation he had created would disappear in about half a day. It would "melt" from the earth, much as a snowbank, starting at the edges and vanishing without a trace. The wrinkle would evaporate into the surrounding atmosphere.

He was curious about the girl, about what would happen when the area around her returned to normal, but he felt an increasing urgency to return to the canyon. He had expended a tremendous amount of energy this day, and he needed some time to rejuvenate. Also, he knew, many humans would be here soon, hunting for the family. He wanted to be safely ensconced in his lair before they came.

So, he headed towards the beckoning rim of the gorge, moving at an easy trot, blithely unaware of the cell phone Audrey had tossed over the wrinkle, landing safely on normal ground on the other side.

CHAPTER 4

The anomaly melted as the power that created it no longer maintained a hold upon it. Slowly the edges receded. Trees and earth that had been misshapen and dead flowed back to life as the phenomenon sank back toward the canyon. One piñon tree stood in bifurcated relief; half of its branches live and green, with the other half still twisted and barren of life. The affected region melted as it receded, and the trees and earth sprang back as if they had been covered with a blanket of desolation and death, which masked, but did not extinguish, the life within.

Audrey lay still and unconscious, unaware of what was happening around her. Slowly the melting effect neared her immobile form. The leading edge of the receding aberration reached Audrey, the effect hesitated as it encountered her body, as if unsure of what to do. The effect continued to disappear from the surrounding terrain, but it lay clinging to Audrey.

Almost as if a conscious decision had been made, the anomaly receded along Audrey's body, taking her physical form with it. Slowly but surely her supine frame melted away, the effect lagging behind the surrounding terrain slightly. A few moments later, the effect erased the last of her corporeal shell, quickly forming a smooth line again as it continued receding towards the distant canyon.

The place where Audrey lay was smooth and unblemished. The dirt and pebbles didn't remember her. It was as if she had ceased to exist, had never existed, and the earth was quiet.

CHAPTER 5

I've been jumpy ever since I had the encounter with Coyote in the parking garage. I still wasn't sure whether he was really there, or if it was some type of manifestation. I've even wondered if I had some type of waking nightmare. Also, I didn't understand the vision I had, or at least not completely. I seemed to be in the body of an ancient Indian, an Anasazi. I felt his worry about the safety of his family, even though they lived in a group of dwellings perched on a ledge, high above the bottom of a canyon. It was impossible anyone, or anything, would be able to attack a place so difficult to reach, except maybe an eagle.

Also, I sensed strangeness about my apartment yesterday. I noticed a funny odor when I came in after work. Everything inside my refrigerator was fine. Still, I was vaguely uneasy, and I just couldn't shake the feeling something was wrong. All my belongings were just as I left them, and I couldn't find any real reason to believe someone had been in my apartment. Just for my own peace of mind, I set up a couple of cameras in different areas. I can access them from my smart phone, so I'll feel a little better coming home after work. On top of that, I decided to kick it old school. I've read lots of spy novels in my day, so I know about putting a hair on top of the door.

I checked the hair and the cameras today and found no sign of intruders. This gave me a much-needed feeling of security, and I'm enjoying my evening at home a lot more than I did the last few days. I watch a little TV, play my computer game for a while, and go to bed a little earlier than usual. I haven't been sleeping that well since I met Coyote downstairs, and I could use some extra to catch up on my "sleep debt."

~ * ~

A hawk circles lazily above him, searching for prey. It is late afternoon in the canyon, and the shadows slowly march across the valley floor, making their inexorable journey up the side of the gorge. As the sun continues to sink lower in the sky, the cliff dwelling also enters shadow, the last remnants of light clinging to outcroppings and treetops, before yielding to the encroaching dark.

 He sits outside the dwelling, safely ensconced on the top of a small ceremonial kiva. He says goodbye to the last rays of the sun, hitting the rim of the canyon far above him, imbuing the white sandstone bluff with a warm pink hue, a brief ambrosia of beauty and the reminder all things pass. He sits patiently, letting the dark settle in around him. He is waiting.

 He hears one coyote. It starts out as a yip, followed shortly by two more yips. Other coyotes join in, one more, followed by another, and another. Soon the yips are replaced by howls, eerie and haunting, harbingers of a pack getting ready to hunt, or perhaps more. It has been a long time, and the man knows He will soon join them on a hunt. It is time to prepare, just in case.

 He enters the kiva, feeling his way down the wooden ladder, feeling each rung through his woven yucca sandals. He makes his way from the entrance, which is in the center of the ceremonial dwelling, to the eastern part of the room, towards the wall. He fumbles and finds the flint and strikes an arc onto the dry grass that is nestled into the fire pit. The sparks catch, and the grass begins to glow. He blows gently, expertly, on the incipient fire, and quickly coaxes a small flame. He adds a few pieces of small kindling, allowing the fire to bloom. Fifteen minutes later, the fire is burning steadily, and he is ready.

 He begins to sing. The words and melody belong to a song that is passed down, from one generation to the next, to one man only. He learned this song, and others, from his father. It is usually done this way. As he sings, he begins to weave a spell of protection about the small village. He summons Snake, for She is the sky, and She protects the entire settlement.

 He places Her head at the entrance to the settlement and traces Her coils in a sinusoidal pattern over the entire open space over the dwellings, creating a protective layer from the ledge on which the village rests, to the rock overhang that stretches above the entire village. He finishes, placing her tail at the far end of the ledge, completing the process. Next, he interweaves Snake, with Bear, whose tracks will scare coyotes away.

 He adds the memory of light, with the love a mother has for her child. This will give strength and courage to the spell. He sprinkles some ground maize onto the fire. This will feed the spell, give the spell sustenance, and the ability to endure.

 Now he is done. Whether this enchantment will be powerful enough to protect them from Him, if He awakens, the man doesn't know. But it does have power. He can feel the spell in the air around him. He banks the fire and waits. Before the fire dies completely, he makes his way to the ladder. He climbs it slowly and clambers out to the top of the kiva. He waits on the kiva's roof, listening. The coyotes' howling has stopped. Satisfied, he gingerly descends the steps carved into a giant boulder and in through the key shaped door to his sleeping family.

~ * ~

I woke up with a start, the memory of the village, the man, filling my mouth, my stomach. It was so real I couldn't believe it was just a dream. Question, if the memory of a dream is just as vivid as any waking memory a person has, didn't it happen? That's the way I felt.

I lay in bed pondering, and impelled by a sudden irresistible urge, I got up and went to my living room, turning on the light. I grabbed my phone and turned on Record. I spoke, recounting the dream. I didn't want to lose it. Sometimes dreams fade away in the light of day, vanishing like a wisp of steam, curling into the air and out of the fabric of reality. I didn't think I'd ever forget this, but I wanted to make sure.

I finished outlining the dream. I hesitated and grabbed a Gatorade® from the refrigerator. I took a few sips, cleared my throat, and sang. Somehow, I wasn't sure why, but I knew this song was important. I finished recording. I listened to it, making sure my voice caught the fluted nuances I remembered so vividly from the dream. I listened to my singing and caught a few places that needed adjusting. I made the adjustments and listened again. It took a few tries, but I was satisfied my song mirrored and caught the spirit of the one in the dream. I put my phone back on the charger, turned off the light, and went back to bed.

~ * ~

I woke early the next morning. I always wake early, even when I have trouble sleeping at night. The afterimage of the dream still circulated through my subconscious, creating a little niggling sensation in the back of my mind. I still found myself pondering it and wondering at its power and clarity.

But duty called, and I knew I needed to start getting ready for work. I pushed thoughts of the dream aside and made myself some coffee. I like reading the news on my laptop while I drink my coffee, and so I was slowly sipping and perusing the various headlines when one byline caught my eye: "FAMILY DISAPPEARS IN CANYON COUNTRY IN SOUTH-EASTERN UTAH," it stated. I immediately was curious and pulled up the article. I read the basic facts; a family of four had vanished without a trace. Their car was at the trailhead, and BLM (Bureau of Land Management) had launched an extensive search, but no sign had been found as yet. Officials surmised they had gotten disoriented in the canyon and were either still wandering and lost or perhaps had succumbed to lack of water and exhaustion.

I did a quick Google search, since they were last seen in the general area where I like to hike. I even thought I might be able to help out due to my knowledge of the area. I found a couple more news items but nothing that gave any additional information.

I asked myself the obvious question. "Does this have any connection to Coyote?"

I had a strong feeling it might. I wasn't sure, of course, but I remembered Coyote's words, how he had told me he was going to wake up, how he hadn't really been awake for a long time. I also remembered his other warning. He had said to never return. I wanted to go back. I needed to know if my actions were somehow responsible for this. If they were, I would have to figure out some way to fix it. Yet his admonition to never return had me worried. I didn't know what he was, but Coyote was not of this earth. Either that or he was much older, a creature left over from the maelstrom at the beginning of the world.

I got to work and talked to the lead tech right away. We're always behind in IT, and even though I had lots of PTO built up, and no one else had the next week off, they didn't want me to take another vacation so soon.

"You need to give more warning when you need some time," my supervisor growled at me. "Unless it's an emergency, we can't afford to let you go. It really puts a big load on the other guys."

The usual BS, in other words. I had to admit that in a way I was relieved. I didn't really want to go back, not right now, anyway. It was heading into late fall right now, and maybe by next spring this whole mess with Coyote, and weird dreams, will have blown over.

Coyote

~ * ~

I did more research on the family when I got home from work. I found it was a husband and wife, with a twelve-year-old daughter and eight-year-old son. The search had been going on for a week already; I just hadn't seen it in the headlines for whatever reason. The officials had opened the trail back up, and the search was winding down, except for a few of the local government guys who were stationed in the area. I kind of felt relieved when I read this. The family really had gotten lost, and it had nothing to do with me. I heaved an inward sigh of relief and made some plans for the weekend with a couple of friends. It'd be good to get out and stop worrying about the whole affair.

A couple of days passed and the weekend approached. I got off work Thursday afternoon, did a little shopping, and headed home. I left the Jeep in the parking garage and went to the elevator. I noticed my jitters were almost gone, and I didn't look over my shoulder even once on the way to the elevator. I hummed a little bit as the elevator made its way to my floor. I was anticipating the weekend. A new escape room was opening in town, and my buddies and I were eager to try it. Maybe it wasn't the type of thing everyone liked to do, but I didn't mind being labeled a Geek.

I got to the door of my apartment, the key in my right hand, a bag of groceries in the other. I opened the door, sat the groceries down on the small table I keep just inside for that reason, and closed and locked it behind me. I stuck the keys in my pocket, picked up the bag, and headed for the kitchen.

I froze. The weird smell was here. It was unmistakable, and it very essence screamed "COYOTE" at me. I sat the groceries down on the couch, absentmindedly. Just like before, everything was in its place. I didn't see anything in the bedroom. The kitchen was clean as well. I thought about going for my gun again but decided against it. No real evidence to indicate someone, or something, had been in my place. There was just that damn smell. I grabbed the groceries and took them into the kitchen. I loaded the fruit and meat into the refrigerator and took out the other few items and stored them in the cupboard. I went back to the bedroom, meaning to change into my sweats. I liked lounging around in them while I was at home. So comfy.

I opened the bedroom door and sat down on the bed, taking off my shoes. I didn't remember where I put my sweats. My gaze strayed over the nightstand by the head of the bed. An object lay on the floor between the nightstand and the wall. Curious, I leaned over and turned on the lamp on the nightstand. The area flooded with light, the darkness fleeing into the corners and niches of the room. Time slowed and stood still. The smell came back suddenly, stronger than before. It assailed my nostrils and disappeared on the wings of the shuddering dark. I was outside of my body, and I watched with curious dispassion as I got up from the bed, knelt by the nightstand and picked up a small sock. It obviously wasn't mine; it had to belong to child. I observed as I turned it over, noticing the dark stain that fragmented the material, sullying the world with blood and evil. I knew, even before I returned to myself, that it belonged to one of the children who had disappeared in Utah a couple of weeks ago.

I stared at the sock dully, in shock. I was unable to think. When the thoughts did come; they were jumbled, a vitriolic mixture of fear, indecision, paranoia, and anger, all thrust into a boiling cauldron of the knowledge Coyote wasn't going to let me go. For now, at least, I was embroiled in an increasingly dangerous and intense game, with no way out.

So, what should I do? This is the question that has plagued me ever since my experience in the canyon. I haven't told anyone about it, for the obvious reasons ("So how was your hiking trip out in the canyon?" "Oh, fine, I saw some dark ritual involving coyotes with some sort of ancient, eldritch coyote god, and now his essence visits me, terrorizing me in my apartment, but good, yeah man, it was good.") Now the stakes are even higher. What am I supposed to do, take this bloody sock, the pure white material now dark and clotted, to the police and tell them a god from our distant past left it in my place? He's got me trapped, and I have to solve the puzzle, it's like the escape room, you have to find the hidden clue, and a secret door will open, yawning its way into a dark path, but one that leads to the way out.

CHAPTER 6

I unlocked the door and turned the handle, gently pushing the door open. Every time I enter my apartment now it's accompanied by a sense of dread, a cold trickle of fear starting at the bottom of my stomach, and slowly seeping into my bowels. I think this is what I hate most of all about what Coyote has done to me. No place is safe place anymore. My home, my sanctuary, has been violated, leaving me with a constant little flicker of fear. It's like a nagging cough you just can't get rid of, always in the back of your mind, and every time you think it's gone away, it reminds you it's still around. I was finally fed up. I was going to have to move. I didn't want to, because I was the kind of guy who gets settled into a place and hates to change, but mostly because I felt like Coyote had beat me. He managed to chase me out of my own house, I felt like a dog who's been whipped by another dog in my own yard. Humiliation brewed inside me as I sought a new place to live.

~ * ~

The townhouse was nice. I told the agent I'd take it. I rounded up my two friends, and they're going to help me move next weekend. I'll owe them, of course, but we always help each other out, and I know it'll even out over time. The main thing, of course, is to change where I live. I need to find out if he can find me. Maybe this will be the end of it.

~ * ~

A month has gone by. It is now winter. I like my new place. It even has a private garage. No more parking garages. Also, there are no elevators; it only has one level, with no one living above me. The sock I found in my bedroom still plagues me, of course. I wonder if I should throw it away or send it to the police anonymously. I can't bear to get rid of it, and so I put it in a zippered plastic bag and bury it behind some papers in a small filing cabinet I have. It also serves to keep it out of my sight, which allows me to think about it less. And so, in this way, fall faded into winter, and the world around me darkened and became cold. Nothing indicated Coyote was visiting me, or even knew where I was. I hoped it was over.

CHAPTER 7

Coyote lounged in his cave. It was light inside, even without any discernable sources of light. Instead, it manifested from the walls of the cavern, a warm, yellow glow suffusing the air and lending a mellow, comfortable feeling to the surroundings. Coyote liked comfort; it wasn't exactly what a human would experience as luxury, but it sufficed for Coyote. He sat on a throne of rock. It was rudely constructed, just some flat sandstone rocks stacked in a way that anyone would recognize as an armchair. It was built against the side of the cave, on the rear wall, far from the entrance. A large stone sat in front, and a nice piece of the flat rock perched upon it, backed up against the side of the cave, which sloped upwards. This formed the seat of the chair, and it was set in a way that allowed it to be reasonably level. Two pieces of flat sandstone set upright adorned each side of the seat. They were thick, and the upper part of these two rocks served as armrests. A large piece of rock was set at the back of the chair, the bottom resting just behind the seat. The rock was set perpendicular to the floor and served as a backrest. All together it had an uncanny resemblance to what could be found in a furniture store, except for the material used to construct it.

Coyote sat on the chair, a black, rectangular device in his hand. He used his finger-pads to expertly swipe the screen. He was using a tablet.

It is very easy to manipulate these devices the humans hold so dear, Coyote mused to himself. He had found the device in the backpack of the adult female they had harvested. He had appropriated it right away, as the ordinary coyotes had no use or need for such a thing and had brought it to his cave to puzzle over. It hadn't taken too long to figure out. Humming at different keys, with different speeds and patterns, he fought with the device for a while, but then he hit on the right note, and his spell took over. After that it was simple enough to convince this "tablet" it had a full battery, even though it was long dead. Also, the password was easy enough to figure out, once he looked closely at the thing. He could see threads of energy inside, and merely followed the thread that led to the inputs for the password. He had figured out the keyboard, and so he played with the tablet, inputting each letter and symbol, and watching the flow of energy. Every time a correct letter or symbol was used, he could see the flow of energy even out, become the same on both sides of the input. Once he figured out each symbol, it opened. Of course he could have sung to it and opened it as well, but this was more fun.

He found the Wi-Fi and internet connections interesting, though at first, he was frustrated by them. He was forced to sing to the machine and let his mind travel with it, until he saw what the functions of this part of the device were. He remembered the strange tower the humans had put up on a nearby mountain several years ago. He could see lines of force coming out of it and had always wondered what they were used for. Now, he suddenly understood. He climbed out of the canyon, easily loping along, using paths and footholds that had existed for thousands of years. He reached the top a short while later, and stood, facing north towards the mountain. The lines of force that emanated from the tower were weaker here, and wide gaps were interspersed between the lines. Coyote looked at the lines and decided to try three. He stepped to his left, reached up, and took a line in his hand-paw. He hummed and sang a soft, soothing melody, one designed to attract. He took the line and slowly coaxed it over to another line, weaving them together. He stepped to his right and did the same to another line of force. Once the three were merged, he took off down into the canyon, pulling them with him as he went. Much as a lineman might unroll a spool of wire, Coyote guided the lines of information from the cell tower to his cave. He stopped at the entrance and gently anchored them to the rocky entrance. He molded a fastening spell with his hand-paw and insured the lines were secured within it. He pulled them across the roof of the cave, finishing at his chair. He hooked the tablet to Wi-Fi and explored the endless possibilities of the internet.

CHAPTER 8

The next couple of months passed, and winter loosened its grip on the land. The days became longer, and in the afternoon the sun gave off a palpable warmth. Spring was coming. I was really enjoying life in the townhouse, and I was looking forward to the warmer weather. I even had a small backyard where I could have my friends over for a barbecue. I felt the experiences of last year fade, the vibrant colors of the memories turning to light pastels, with no real power or urgency behind them.

Then, I got a bitter reminder Coyote hadn't forgotten about me. I came home Saturday afternoon. My friends and I tried out a board game café. It was lots of fun, especially because of a table of girls next to us. We talked, and I hit it off with one of them. She was really into reading and sci-fi and fantasy. We had arranged to meet for a coffee/game date later in the week. I was really relishing the future. I entered my apartment with my whole-body kind of humming. It had been a really good day.

I'm socially awkward, so meeting this girl was really important for me. I don't get that many opportunities and often they somehow hit a snag. I just don't have any luck with women, and I remembered what had happened a few months previous.

I met her at a trade show. It featured electronic items, which was perfect for me. I always love seeing what's coming out, what's new. One of the new GPS units that's used for hiking, for example. I like carrying a unit with me when I go out in the desert and hike, especially since I'm usually alone. I had picked up this unit and was trying out the various menus, seeing how cool it was, and the different ways of planning routes and loving the graphic interface, when I felt someone behind my shoulder.

I glanced over towards my left, wondering who it was, and was somewhat shocked to see a pretty girl curiously checking out the unit I was holding.

"Wow," she exclaimed, as she checked out the gear in my hands, "that's great." Then she looked up at me in a manner both guileless and full of curiosity.

I noticed vivid blue eyes. I'm not really used to talking to beautiful girls. I unfroze and managed to awkwardly answer her. "Yeah, it's really neat. I'm thinking about getting it for my hiking trips."

"Hiking?" she responded avidly. "Oh, that's so cool. I love hiking!"

She kept her eyes locked on me. I felt hypnotized, and somehow, someway, I felt myself opening up and able to talk to her, which usually doesn't happen.

"Yeah, hiking's really great. So, do you just go around here, or do you go to the mountains?"

"I go to the mountains whenever I can, but there are some decent trails around here. I just like to get out, you know. I like the way I feel after a good workout."

I couldn't believe it: this girl gave off clues of being interested. I could tell she was really engaged in the conversation, and I noticed she was toying with her hair. I'd done enough reading on the subject to know this was an indication of attraction.

Then she moistened her lips with her tongue and reached out, putting her hand lightly on my shoulder. "Nice talking with you," she said and turned and walked away.

I hesitated for minute, in consternation, I had hoped we were going to talk a little more, and I already had some thoughts on trying to ask her out.

"Hey, wait," I blurted impulsively and stepped after her.

"Oh, sure," she said brightly, turning back around immediately, her eyes piercing me once again.

"So, maybe we should go hiking together sometime," I mumbled unconvincingly.

"Sure," she responded casually, "sounds like fun."

"So, do you want to trade numbers?" I ventured doubtfully.

"Actually," she said immediately, "why don't we meet down at the place that sells hiking stuff across town? They've got a really great wall for climbing?"

"Sure, okay," I replied hopefully. I'd been a couple of times, and I knew about their wall. "Does Saturday at eleven work for you?"

"Saturday…hmmm, how about eleven thirty?"

"Sure," I replied somewhat eagerly. "Yeah, eleven thirty's

fine."

"Oh, and I'm Anne, by the way," she said somewhat pointedly.

"Oh, oh yeah, yeah," I responded, somewhat embarrassed. "I'm Jim, nice to meet you. I guess I forgot about the name thing," I finished somewhat lamely.

She smiled at me, and I could tell she found my shyness a little charming. "See you then," she said and sailed off, her lithe form disappearing rapidly between the various tables and displays at the show.

It was really nice at first. The problem was I don't get many opportunities to date, and so I agonize over every little detail. I spent the next couple of days obsessing over everything and fantasizing about having someone like Anne as a girlfriend.

For me, that would be quite an accomplishment.

Then the day came, and I met her down at the wall. She acted happy to see me, but it turned out she'd brought a couple of friends with her, a couple of male friends. I was pretty disappointed, but I was determined to play out my hand. The climbing did go well, and I enjoy climbing a lot, so I was able to hang in there with the three of them pretty easily.

Then I felt a desire to show up the other two guys, kind of stupid, I know, but I couldn't help the feelings, and so I climbed the most difficult part of the wall, determined to show I could outdo them. When I made it to the part where the wall actually leans out a little bit, for professional level climbers only, I couldn't resist the urge to rub it in on the two guys a little bit, and I guess I overdid it. All three of them were a little bit quiet and withdrawn, and when we got a table at a nearby place and ordered some drinks, they talked amongst themselves, leaving me out.

I hated this. It was a perfect example of my life. I was there but not there. An invisible barrier excluded me from their circle. I took out my phone and pretended I was busy texting my friends. This went on for a bit, and then the one guy left. It got a bit better after that, when we talked about climbing and the trade show, and I felt included. Then the other guy excused himself, and Anne and I were left alone at the table. Awkward silence prevailed, one of those times when the discomfort was a tangible thing, turning the air around us into a solid block of ice, freezing us into contorted caricatures of our former selves. I was determined to act, though, and even though it felt horribly wrong, I went ahead and asked her for her number. (I know lots of people use social media to hit up others or to initiate a friendship, but I'm kind of old-fashioned, I guess. I prefer a number to text or even call.)

She seemed reluctant, and I was surprised when she ended up giving it to me. I was happy with the win, and when the other guy showed back up, I made my excuses and headed out. I'd got what I came for and didn't see any point hanging around any longer. I wanted to see if I could get her to go out on an actual date with me.

That's when the usual problems escalated. I texted her later that day and told her I'd really enjoyed the afternoon. She didn't get back to me for a while, but a few hours later she texted back saying it had been nice. I took this as a good sign and texted her back right away, but she didn't answer that day. The next day I texted her again, and she responded a few hours later. I went ahead and called her, determined to ask her out, to close the deal.

As she was friendly enough on the phone, after a minute or so of small talk, I asked her if she'd go to dinner with me. She didn't actually say yes or no, and so I forged ahead, trying to get an answer out of her, one way or the other. She told me she was really busy studying for a test, some type of professional certification. I got excited then, because I'm good at taking tests. I offered to help her study, I thought this would be the perfect way to show her I'd be a good guy to have around.

She wasn't nearly as receptive to the idea as I thought she'd be. She said she preferred to study alone, and when I pointed out that interacting with another person and responding to questions was more in line with the actual test experience, she reluctantly agreed. I just couldn't pin her down on an actual time to get together though, and I found myself becoming frustrated. I gave up and ended the conversation, with some vague plans of maybe getting together someday but nothing concrete. I would never be getting together with her. She just wasn't interested in me. I don't understand, I always try so hard, and it never gets me anywhere.

CHAPTER 9

I unlocked the door and stepped inside. I instinctively closed and locked the door, then froze. My essence catapulted from humming with joy and anticipation to shivering with dread with a sick feeling in my stomach. The peculiar odor delicately hovered in the air about me, a whiff of pungent earth and a cruel animal like stench that permeated the room. I lurched forward, not bothering to be careful. I checked the bedroom and the bathroom. I didn't see anything unusual. In the kitchen, the odor was strongest. I opened each cabinet door and all the drawers. I didn't see anything. I opened the refrigerator. Again, nothing was unusual, nothing out of place or new. I felt relief: maybe the smell was just a gas leak, and my imagination was working overtime.

I froze and went back to the cabinets. I opened each one, taking an inventory of the contents. I pulled on the knob on the third door, releasing the magnetic latch. This is where I kept my pancake and cornbread mixes. Ensconced between my usual brands was a new box. I reached in and pulled it off the shelf. I read the title slowly, to myself, "Coyote Pancake & Waffle Mix." I'd never heard of such a thing, and certainly hadn't purchased it. Coyote was sending me a message.

"Why does it have to happen like this?" I said to myself. "Just when things were going so good."

Part of me was bitter, another frightened. I was beginning to understand: Coyote wasn't going to forget about me, and I was going to have to figure out some way of fighting back.

I did the only thing I knew how to do—and I'm really good at it. I hit the books. I did the obvious, a Google search on Coyote mythology and ancient gods. It didn't take long to find out lots of interesting information. Various Native American tribes have a long and rich history concerning coyotes. Some believe in a Coyote god who is older than the world itself. They believe he was present at the creation of the earth, and he will be here, still alive, when the earth crumbles and dies. This was all interesting and eye-opening stuff, the only problem with it being—they were describing a being that is outside of time and has no weaknesses, or at least none mentioned.

So, am I going to have to fight an all-powerful, immortal being? Maybe he'll be like Smaug, with a little tender spot under one armpit. Regardless, he has some way of tracking me. So, I must decide, fight or flight. It's easy to find jobs in IT, so I could move much farther from canyon country. I could even go overseas. I have to decide, and soon.

I got up and enjoyed an obligation-free Sunday as much as I could, under the circumstances. I didn't have any real plans so just hung out around the house and interspersed my computer game with more research on the Coyote mythos. Monday came and back to work. The day passed quickly. Always lots of problems happen at work after days off. The network seems self-aware, and it always picks my days off to manifest several issues the people who work weekends have to deal with. I spent the day trying to restore the company's intranet to a wing of the building, along with other smaller problems different users had reported.

I headed home. Usually, I'd relax for a few hours after a hard day, but now I was paranoid, worried about some new article lying around my place. I parked the Jeep and walked over to the mail area. I received mail with other tenants in a cluster of boxes, a couple of them being larger to hold parcels. I would get a key in my personal box in case of a package for me.

I opened my personal box, dug through the junk mail and such and saw the key. I grabbed it curiously. I didn't remember ordering anything lately. I like online shopping, and so it wasn't out of the question that something was waiting for me that somehow escaped my memory. Kind of a "surprise gift" to myself. I opened the larger metal door. Wrapped in brown paper was a package. It was roughly the size of a book; I reached down and picked it up. It was the right size and weight for a hardback, and I loved ordering books. I closed the metal door and went home. I dumped the junk mail and package on my couch. I sniffed the air and was relieved to note it was clean, no visitations today. I made a beeline to the kitchen and made coffee. I would drink it and relax while catching up on the latest TV series that I was binge watching. The coffee brewed, and I went back into the living room. I tossed the junk mail into the recycle bin. I believe in recycling.

I picked up the mystery package and unwrapped it: a

hardback book. The brown dust jacket revealed itself, gently materializing into a distinct form. I suddenly felt a surrealistic wave wash over the room. I reached down and turned the book over, exposing the title. *Coyote Waits* by Tony Hillerman. I knew this book well; in fact, I had a copy in the back room with my other books. I knew I had not ordered it. I tried to find the shipping address. I sifted through the torn shreds of paper, so like my life, with no return address. No stamps, and not even my name and address. The paper was devoid of any information, offering no clue as to how it had got into the box or how the mail carrier had decided it was for me and had deposited it.

Coyote Waits. I knew what he meant. He was waiting for me.

CHAPTER 10

Spring came to the desert. It was only the early part of March, but the winter snow was already a faded memory, the distant mountain peaks still white and frozen a mere cobweb of a reminder that the land had been cold and still. The piñon and juniper stood vibrant and green, and the small groups of holly that inhabited the dark shady areas shouted with joy at the beginning of a new year. The cottonwoods slowly emerged from the dark, their gray sinister branches turning green and elegant, redolent with life and hope. The cactus awakened, their drooping branches turning stiff and attentive, and small buds developed, the promise and hope of the continuation of life.

A new, fresh beginning infected the people in the area as well, and as the trails dried and the days grew warm, they filtered into the desert. A few may have remembered the family that disappeared the previous fall, but if they did it was a mere flash of unease that briefly appeared in their thoughts and vanished to be replaced with the joy of the celebration of life that is spring.

It didn't take long. Coyote was awake now and with this the thirst to hunt, to find and slowly squeeze the fear of his prey into the refreshing, if somewhat decadent, screams of their deaths, pervaded his will.

A young couple appeared shortly, and he watched as they dropped down into the canyon, their young, athletic limbs easily conquering the narrow, steep cleft that guarded the entrance to the easier trail below. He waited until they reached the bottom of the gorge; he set his will to the land, and soon they ran with no place to go, and he and his cohorts fed on them. He smoothed and cleaned the area. The couple vanished from this world, leaving no trace but the harrowing memory shared by their family and friends.

~ * ~

I was at work, having lunch with my colleagues at the small cafeteria we have for our use. I was surfing the net on my phone, the same as my co-workers, when I saw the headline. COUPLE

Coyote

DISAPPEARS IN SOUTHEAST UTAH. I pulled up the article. They had parked at the same trailhead as the family last fall. The news agency was doing its usual thing, trying to put a sinister spin on it, but this time I had a feeling they were right. This time it was a monster. It was just a lot worse than they knew.

I went home and considered my options. I was still in fight or flight mode, and I just couldn't decide what to do. I was sure a trip to the canyon would be the end of me. I had no plan, no idea how to defeat Coyote. I messed around with my computer game, but just couldn't concentrate. I thought about texting the girl I'd met, but right now I just couldn't see it. Any other time I would have been excited, but now I couldn't focus on anything but Coyote. I gave up and went to bed early.

I tossed and turned, sleep evading me, smoothly eluding my grasp, like water slipping through fingers. I checked the clock periodically, the red numbers slowly counting, and wondered if I was going to have to go work tomorrow with zero sleep. Ten, eleven, midnight, time marched on, the one inexorable facet of our existence. Somewhere close to one in the morning, I drifted off to sleep.

~ * ~

My shoulders shook as I wept; sorrow and impotent rage suffused my being. The tears, bitter and useless, poured from my eyes. Why, oh why, didn't she listen to me? My daughter, light of my life, gone, taken by him. I thought back to the day before, my mind whirling as I tried to figure out what I had done wrong, where my mistake lay.

We were at the fields, down in the bottom of the canyon. It was a beautiful day, and we praised the earth for granting us this day. The men and women tended the maize, each person armed with a hoe made of sandstone, ruthlessly attacking the weeds that threatened the mainstay of our existence. One young man was posted at each corner of the field, standing high up in the watchtowers we had built, their sharp eyes constantly searching for any sign of the enemy. Any sign of a coyote requires caution, for we have learned his presence is always presaged by the sighting of one of his lesser brethren. The children ran and played among us. The older ones are already learning to care for the maize. The younger ones are given the freedom to spend their days carefree and full of joy. This is a gift our people hold sacred: that the young ones pass their days without worry or fear. The gift of their presence to us is thus reflected back to them. This is the way all things must be, the way it has been for countless years.

Breela, or bird, is my daughter. She is my favorite, and though all children are precious, she is special in every way. I smiled to myself as I toiled with the maize, the sounds of her happy laughter swelling in my heart, until I thought it would burst. This was the last summer for her to be child. I knew that soon the flowing of the sands of time would propel her forward, and she would become a young woman. Not yet though, not just yet, she still had time to be a child.

I continued to work in the field, and my mind moved to other issues. Would the crop this year be sufficient to comfortably feed us the next winter? Would the earth be merciful? These and other issues weigh on me, for as "The one who knows the songs," I have a responsibility not only to myself, but the whole tribe.

I was ripped out of my reverie. The laughter had died, torn asunder from this world and whipped away by the cruel winds of destiny. I tried to figure out what was wrong. All seemed well; my brothers and sisters still toiled beside me, working as one to bring our crops to fruition. Four watchtowers were dutifully manned, the young men alertly casting their sharp gaze throughout the canyon, looking for trouble. And yet something was wrong. It was the children. They had disappeared; the field was silent, bereft of life and joy. I called out to the nearest watchtower.

"Honti, where are the children?" I asked, a catch in my voice.

He anxiously cast about for them.

"They were here just moments ago," he answered, confusion in his heart. "I don't understand what happened to them. I don't remember seeing them go."

Honti called out to the other towers, cupping his hands around his mouth and using his height above ground to make his voice carry: "Ho, Brisho, Marog, Kronti, do you see the children?"

All the men uneasily looked around them. First apprehensive and then feverish, they searched the area around the field. My brothers and sisters stopped their work, uneasy. Shifting from lightly apprehensive to deeply concerned, we all called and searched for the children.

Brisho hailed us: "I see them, they're almost out of sight, up at the bend of the canyon."

I ran, leaving the field and the work behind me. The young men flew past me, rushing to get to the children. Moments later the whole tribe arrived at the canyon bend. The children were acting strangely. They seemed confused and didn't remember leaving the fields. They weren't frightened or repentant. They were in a trance. They reminded me of the way people say I act when I sing a spell. Here but not quite here—it's the only way to put it.

We counted the children, choking with fear as we checked off their names. Soon most of them were accounted for, almost all safe, save one. Breela was missing. She was not with the others, and I knew she was taken because of me. Coyote is trying to break me, to weaken the protection that guards me and my family.

I face the blank canyon walls, empty and desolate, just like the rest of my life will be. I raise my hands above my head and scream, a cry of inarticulate and passionate rage. I would bring the whole canyon down on all of us; I would crush all my brothers and sisters if it would serve to bring her back.

~ * ~

I woke from the dream with tears on my cheeks. I had been crying. It had been over two months since the last dream about this man, and this one was more vivid and much more personal than the others. His desolation and loss still coursed through me. I felt as though I had tasted the life of another being. It was five AM. I usually get up early anyway, and I knew I would never sleep again this night, not after what I had experienced. So, I got up and prepared for the coming day.

I was distracted and moody at work that day. Fortunately, I had some work to do that I could do solo, and so I told my boss where I'd be and went to take care of it. I really didn't want to talk to anyone, or be around anyone. I just wanted to think about the dream. I felt it was one of those moments in life when you're touched in such a profound way you will never be quite the same afterward. I did the work by rote, and the day slipped away, much as our lives, into the past.

I came home still somewhat distracted. I opened the door and stepped into the living room. I tossed my keys on the table, and headed for the kitchen, as I usually do. A small noise, like scratching against the wall, interrupted my reverie. It came from the bedroom. I still wasn't thinking straight, and I just switched my path from the kitchen to the bedroom, opening the door and barging in.

I stopped in shock, and fear. Coyote stood before me,

across the room on the other side of my bed. He grinned at me. He extended his paw-arm, without speaking, and held an object out towards me. He let it dangle and slowly swung it from side to side, like the pendulum on a grandfather clock. I was automatically focused on it, and with a rush of fear I realized it was a pair of women's underwear, the white cotton kind someone might wear for athletic activity, or maybe if they were going for a long hike. The panties were splotched and crusted with a dark reddish-brown substance. I knew, without thinking, it was blood.

Coyote stopped swinging the macabre reminder of violence and death and spoke. "Come see me," he said gently, "or these are going to be "found" in your apartment soon."

"What are you talking about?" I stuttered. "How do you keep finding me?"

"Your internet is an interesting invention," he replied. "It's rather easy to use, and I can find you now, no matter where you go."

How in the hell does this creature know about the internet? I found myself wondering, as I faced him.

"Why do you want me to come see you?" I asked. "Why don't you just leave me alone?"

He smiled at me, a baleful, ravenous mockery of what a smile is supposed to convey. He responded.

"I'm going to kill you, of course," he said. "I told you already, you have seen what is forbidden. It was not for humans to see."

Desperately hoping to bargain, I said, "I haven't told anyone what I saw, and even if I did, they'd never believe me. Just let me go. You told me to never come back and I won't, I swear. You don't have anything to worry about."

"Worry," he responded in a mocking superior tone. "I'm not worried at all. I've just decided I want to kill you. Come back to the canyon, or I'll see to it these," he waggled the panties meaningfully, "get found. I did some reading, and I'm sure you wouldn't want to go to prison with the label of a sexual predator, now would you."

He winked at me and doffed his hat and bowed. With a slight pop, he disappeared from the room, leaving no trace behind, except my ravaged soul.

Coyote

~ * ~

I decided I wasn't going to wait for another "present" to somehow appear in my townhouse. I talked to my supervisor the next day and scheduled a week of vacation, starting the week after next. It was the earliest they would let me go. It was okay, because I needed some time to prepare.

I went through all of my gear. I charged my Garmin and got my gun in order.

I updated all my foodstuff and checked my pack. I wasn't really sure what would happen, but I knew I couldn't wait day after day, jumping every time my phone rang or I saw a police officer. I had to take action. The only course left was the canyon. Coyote had trapped me, boxing me into a corner, just as surely as if I were on a point of land on the rim of the canyon, with no avenue of escape except straight down.

I decided to just go to the trailhead with my gear and get a sense for what was happening. I arrived on Saturday about noon, and everything was quiet, normal. My Jeep was the only car at the trailhead, and so I locked the doors and pocketed the key. I gathered my backpack, put it on and adjusted my straps for maximum comfort then headed down the trail, toward the canyon.

I wasn't sure what it was I wanted, or even if I would find anything, but I knew I had to try. I descended the trail slowly, sweeping my gaze back and forth for anything out of the ordinary. I slowly made my way toward the rim, making occasional forays out from the trail. I had made it about halfway to the canyon rim when a light flashed to my right, about one hundred yards off the path. The sun was at the perfect angle when I passed by, or I wouldn't have seen it. It was a reflection off a mirror. I was curious, and so I made my way towards the area where I had spotted it.

It only took a few minutes to walk over to the area. It was typical of the whole terrain in this part of the land, with a sizeable growth of piñon and juniper trees, interspersed with sage brush, and lots of open area. The spot where I had seen the reflection was on a small arm of land that was slightly higher than the surrounding ground. The arm grew in width as it headed south towards the gorge that lay beyond. It tapered and merged into the surrounding landscape as it approached the trail. I prowled around, seeking anything that might cause a reflection. I thought maybe there were some agate deposits on the small uplift, and maybe some of them had crystal growths on the surface, which could reflect sunlight. I didn't find anything that suggested agate deposits.

I rounded a small piñon tree, which stood about ten feet from the edge of the small uplift. I gasped: a cell phone. I picked it up and tried to turn it on. It was dead, so I hurried back to my Jeep, where I could plug it in and turn it on.

As soon as I got to the Jeep, I pulled my USB cable out of the middle console, found the port and connected it. I plugged the other end into the phone, which luckily happened to use the same type of interface as my mobile. The phone immediately buzzed and showed charging. I turned on the power and watched it boot up. I didn't really have much hope that I could get into it, but I figured it was worth a quick try.

The phone booted up and came on. I slid the screen with my finger, and to my astonishment the phone screen came up. It wasn't password protected. A picture of a girl with reddish hair and freckles appeared on the screen. I knew it must belong to the girl who had disappeared.

I struggled with knowing I should take it to the nearest authorities, and the desire to see what was on it. I wavered, but decided to take a quick check. After all, it was hours to town, and by the time I arrived, turned it in, and they mounted any type of response, it would be dark. If something important showed up, I might be able to go back and make a difference before nightfall. I decided it was worth the risk.

I scrolled through the phone. Without a signal here, I didn't try to check emails. A saved draft sat right at the top. The message was heartbreaking, something about a twisted landscape and coyotes. I knew now Coyote was somehow responsible.

I also knew I wanted to get back to the area where I found the phone and do a quick search. I knew the girl and her family must be dead, but I had a feeling searching the area might be important.

I jogged back down the trail, doing a quick-jog-fifty-steps, walk-fifty-steps. This is considered by many to be one of the best programs for fitness, and I use it. It didn't take long to cover the distance back to where I found the phone. This time I moved to the place where I'd picked it up very carefully, studying it for any sign of tracks. I knew the authorities would probably be upset with me, no matter what, but I would try to minimize my "footprint" in the area.

I didn't see any sign of footprints. In fact, the whole uplift was totally devoid of any type of tracks at all. This is unusual, since rabbits and deer roam the area every day, and some type of spoor is usually present. I crossed over the hill and a small clear area directly across the uplift from the place where I'd found the phone. This area abutted the uplift, and it was a little bit unusual, with no plant life growing at all. I carefully circled the cleared area. I got an eerie, chilly feeling, but discovered no sign of any tracks here either.

The dirt across the circle was unnaturally smooth and free of the usual debris and such that clutters the terrain in most wooded areas.

It was very strange, and a little sinister. I just couldn't shake the unease. I decided to cross the uplift and go back over to the place around where I found the phone.

I moved slowly across the rise, sweeping the area carefully. I reached the midpoint without seeing anything. Then I caught something, just out of the corner of my eye. I couldn't figure out what it was, a white object lay on the ground between a couple of trees. As I neared the spot where I had seen the object, I couldn't find anything. I circled both trees, finding nothing. I decided to go back to where I had spotted the object. I returned and stared directly at the spot between the two trees. I couldn't see anything, it was weird, because I knew I had spotted something, just a few moments before.

I backtracked a few paces, going back towards the small, cleared area and strolled forward. I would take a step and stop and observe. Then another step and observe. I finally reached the spot where I had initially seen it. There was nothing. I couldn't believe it. I turned my head back towards the other side of the rise and took a step forward.

I glimpsed it again, out of the corner of my eye! Briefly, a white object, definitely discernible, lay between the two trees, not twenty feet from me. I turned but again, it was gone. I understood the problem. I turned back, facing forward, with the spot just in the corner of my eye. I spotted it again. It was a definite form, lying between the trees. It was ghostly white, but as I grew accustomed to seeing it, I could make out that it was vaguely human in shape.

I had no idea why I could see this thing from the corner of my eye only. Maybe the wavelengths in the visible spectrum are different from that aspect. All I knew for sure was someone lay between those trees.

I knelt down, right by where the body should be. I tentatively moved my hand forward, waiting to meet some type of resistance. Nothing happened: my hand passed through empty air. I passed my hand through the general area around where I thought the body was and encountered empty air. I considered and came up with no explanation for what I could see and no reason why I couldn't touch it a body.

A sudden spark of intuition hit me. I needed to start thinking outside the "box" my world had shaped around me. I reasoned, *in my world, a creature like Coyote can't exist*. Therefore, the answer to all of this must lie beyond the realm of my world and the rules and constrictions I knew so well.

This gave me an idea. I always carry my phone in my pack in case I want to take a picture. I reached into the pack and pulled it out. I rested against a tree and listened to the description of the spell I recorded that night. I listened to the song I had also put on the phone. I played the melody, and I didn't recognize my own voice as the song poured out of the speakers of my mobile and suffused the surrounding air with its ancient call of eldritch power.

The song ended, and I thought I felt the earth tremble under me.

Suddenly I knew what to do.

I found a flat, rectangular rock and pushed one end into the ground, forming the rest of the rock standing perpendicular to the ground. I gathered small, dry twigs. I scooped out a small hole in front of the rock and placed them inside. I pulled out my lighter and set the twigs burning. I gathered some larger branches, and when the fire crackled, I did the ritual.

I visualized a cliff dwelling I had visited many years ago. This dwelling had, still intact on the ceiling above it, a pictograph of a blue snake whose head guarded the entrance of the cave on one side. The body stretched across the entire ceiling, finishing with the tail on the other side of the group of small buildings. I sang the song from the dream, adding Snake—she who protects—to the song. In my mind I drew her above me, encapsulating a small, circular dome on the ground in front of me that extended in a circle about ten feet in diameter, creating a shield from the outside world around me and the body.

Next, I thought about another cliff dwelling I visited only a few years ago. This one had several petroglyphs of bear tracks, the prints beautifully detailed and inscribed on the wall, tracing their way across the rock, alternating between front and back feet, just as a bear would naturally ramble in the forest. I took the tracks and added them to the song, interweaving them with Snake. The bear tracks would also protect, for coyotes were afraid of bears.

I was a little hazy about the memory of light. I couldn't think of anything that allowed a personal connection to this. I thought of a time, about ten years ago, when I had been driving home from work. It was December and snowing hard. The roads were treacherous and icy. Dark comes early on a snowy day in the middle of winter, and the sky was already beginning to dim, the gathering dark rapidly snuffing out the last remnants of the day. A car sat parked on the shoulder, with an elderly lady in it.

A sudden impulse made me pull my car over, parking in front of her. I got out and went over to the front door of her car. She rolled down the window, and I asked if she was okay.

"The car just stopped," she answered. "I didn't know what to do."

"Any place I can take you?" I asked.

"Yes," she replied. "My husband is at home. Could you drive me? It's only a few miles."

"Sure," I said. "No problem. Hop in."

It wasn't until she was in the car that I understood how important my gesture had been.

"The car wouldn't start. I didn't know what to do. No one was stopping."

She must have been very frightened. The fear and

indecision had somehow paralyzed her, and she was unable to call, or wave down a car. What was an insignificant act for me was a monumental one for her. I took her to her house, and she fervently thanked me.

If I were asked to point out one instance in my life that was pure and utterly altruistic, with no thought or hint of an ulterior motive, this would be it. Memory of light, an action done for another with no expectation of any type of reward or acknowledgement. I added this to the spell, hoping it would be enough.

After that came the last part of the enchantment. I remembered visiting my mother in the hospital. She was dying and in pain. Yet when I came to visit, she would always ask me about my day and my life, showing me, even now, she was interested and cared, that she put my needs above her own. A mother's love for her child, the strongest and most enduring force on this earth. I faltered as I remembered, and tears came to my eyes, but I reached out, found my center, and continued. I added this love to the song, gently intertwining it with the existing layers, using it to bind together the protective forces of Snake and Bear, and melding it with the memory of light to give it strength and purpose.

As I completed this binding, the earth behind me suddenly screamed. I was deep in a trance like state, but the rasping, ragged sound brought me near to the surface, and I paused singing and turned.

It came from the unusual circle of earth I noticed earlier. Dirt erupted violently in the mid part of the circle, and clods and small pieces of the terrain were strewn about, as if a small bomb had exploded under the ground, rending it asunder. I was bewildered by the scene. The earth was settling back: whatever had happened was complete.

Some type of entity, pale white to the point of translucence, hovered over the circle. Its form was indeterminate, but roughly circular, and about three feet in diameter. The entity was motionless, but then it found its way.

It rushed at me, charging like a maddened animal. It roared up the small slope, with a deafening speed.

It wasn't charging at me. Instead, it was rushing to the side of the body that lay next to me. The entity abruptly stopped its rush and hovered in the air, a sense of absolute intensity about it as it focused on the area where the body lay.

I recovered and continued singing. As I sang, I pulled a trail mix bar out of my pack. Gently I broke it into four equal portions. The spell had to have sustenance. I placed a portion on each side of the fire, one to the north, the south, the east, and the west. As the spell was ready, I completed the song and the enchantment, and I fell silent.

~ * ~

After a time, the spell coalesced about me. I felt a great peace lightly settle on everything in the protective circle, myself, the trees and the earth itself, the entity, and…the body as well.

The spell took root in the earth itself and exerted its effect on the form beside me. A glow softly appeared, outlining the place where the body lay. Slowly but surely the light grew, gaining strength as it evoked the memory of life into the girl. The soft glow transformed into a shining radiance of steel and fire. Brief whorls of iridescence briefly played and shifted about the body.

The light faded. The luminous effect abated, and I noticed it wasn't merely fading away; it was actually being absorbed into the body of the girl. Soon, the universe cracked, the effects of the spell were ripped asunder, and everything within the circle returned to normal.

One thing was different, however. Now a girl lay before me. She could have been about twelve, with auburn hair and freckles. She was lying on her side, with her eyes closed. Dressed in blue jeans and a long-sleeved shirt, with a knapsack clinging to her back, she seemed to have just settled down moments before, even though I knew she must have been there for several months. I reached out and lightly touched her forehead with the back of my hand. It was warm, and I could see she was alive, just unconscious or sleeping.

The after-effects of the spell casting caught up to me, and I was suddenly exhausted. I grabbed my pack and leaned it up against the nearest tree. I settled into it, using it as a pillow, and faded into an intense, dreamless sleep.

CHAPTER 11

I awoke slowly, sleep dragging its heels, trying to claw my waking being back into slumber. The hand shaking my shoulder was persistent though, and I came to, blearily staring at the person in front of me.

"Wake up mister, wake up," the girl urged me.

"Okay, okay, enough," I protested, groaning as I fought myself into alertness.

I shook my head, clearing the last cobwebs out. She was a regular girl, meeting my gaze directly. It was easy to see she was an open, confident person. Lots of thoughts went on in my head, and I'm sure hers as well.

Her gaze changed, it turned "inward" in a way that spoke volumes about her experiences. Not only was her family gone, but she had also been "elsewhere" for a few months. I couldn't even begin to guess where she had been or what she had experienced.

Her introspective gaze continued, and I could see she wasn't really here, not right now.

"You brought me back," she said softly, in a distracted fashion. It was as if the fact wasn't important.

"Mommy helped you," she said matter-of-factly, as if she were asking me to pass the salt. "She's gone now though."

I thought of the entity that burst from the ground during the spell. *That must have been her mother.* I wondered about the clearing, what exactly had happened.

"Do you know where your family is?" I asked hesitantly.

The girl nodded towards the clearing. "The coyotes... Coyote got them," she said, a brief, hurt note entering her voice.

"Coyote?" I asked, all my senses suddenly sharp and on edge.

"That's what I call it," she replied. It was an animal; similar to a coyote, but on two legs, it wore a funny jacket and hat."

So, it was the same creature that's been after me. I felt a hatred of this thing start to build, as I realized how ruthless, how cruel, he really was.

I trembled with sadness and sympathy, thinking about what

the girl must have seen.

I had to ask though, I had to know more.

"So, what happened to you?" I queried. "How did you manage to escape?"

"The coyotes had us cornered. Coyote was somehow creating these places with the funny trees, and if you tried to enter it felt like millions of razors cutting you. Mom got me to the edge of this place and shoved me inside. I tried to run but passed out."

I had to ask one more question. "So, do you know you've been missing for over three months?" I asked. "Where have you been all this time?"

"I didn't know how long I was gone," she replied. "But I was in a dark place. Everything was black and made of smooth glass. There was no light at all, and it was a city. I just wandered the streets between all these huge skyscrapers. Nobody else was there."

"Wow," I said. "You must have been really scared."

"No," she answered. "Fear doesn't exist where I was. There's no pain, no happiness. There's just…nothing. It felt like I could have been walking those streets for thousands of years, or only an hour. It's hard to explain."

She grew quiet again. "It's where Coyote gets the thing where he changes the trees and stuff. He draws it from that world and pours it into this one. When it went back, it took me with it."

"Changes the trees?" I asked. "What do you mean?"

"We were hiking, and suddenly the trees changed. Everything turned from color to black and white. The branches of the trees were twisting and shaking. It's like they were in pain. The trees were dead, with no leaves, and their branches were all bent out of shape. Dad tried to go into the trees, but when you try to go into them you feel like you're being cut to pieces. That's how I got away. Mommy helped me. She pushed me into the trees. I thought I was going to die: they just kept cutting and cutting. I tried to make it through; I was running as fast as I could. I could see the other side, but I just couldn't make it. It hurt too much."

She stopped, and I could see she was overcome, her face twisted in pain from a memory that was still too near.

I hesitated, torn between emotions. I wanted to comfort her but wasn't sure what to do. I spoke, hoping it was the right thing.

"I'm really sorry about your family," I said, trying to speak normally, to keep the tears forming in my mind out of my voice.

"Thanks," she said simply, and I could see she was elsewhere once again.

"My name's Jim, by the way, and you must be Audrey. I read about you in the news. Is that right?"

"Yes, I'm Audrey," she replied woodenly.

I changed the subject. "Do you have any relatives back home?" I asked. "We need to get back to town. People need to know you're still alive. I'm not too sure what we're going to tell them," I said rather lamely. "I don't think it would be a good idea to tell them the truth about what happened to you, or how I found you. That might make it really complicated for the both of us." (Actually, I have to admit I was thinking it might make it really complicated for me.)

"Maybe it would be better if we just told them you ran away from home. Then we could say I recognized you from the news, and picked you up," I said hopefully.

Audrey stared at me square in the eye. "No," she said. "That's not what we're going to do at all."

The inward glaze returned to her eyes. Audrey wasn't just a little girl anymore. She was something else as well.

She continued, "I've got business down there," she said, indicating the canyon rim in the distance. "I WANT COYOTE'S ASS."

She adjusted her own pack, which was still sitting faithfully on her shoulders, just like it had been for the past few months, and she headed for the trail. I felt indecision as I watched her go. I knew more about Coyote now, and he was extremely dangerous. Nonetheless, I had a sinking feeling as I watched the young girl heading for the canyon alone. I just couldn't let her go by herself. So, I walked rapidly after her to make up the distance she had already covered as she set out for the canyon and whatever it was that awaited us below.

~ * ~

I caught up to her, and I decided to try talk her out of it.

"What are you doing?" I asked her, my voice carrying a high, incredulous note. "Come on, let's get you out of here. At least let me take you to town."

Audrey just glanced at me, a withering sideways glance, and didn't even bother to respond. If anything, she picked up her pace a little.

"So, what's your plan?" I asked. "Do you think you're going down in the canyon, grabbing that monster by the tail, and dragging him to the nearest police station?"

I hoped she would recognize how dangerous this was and change her mind.

"And where are you going? Do you have any idea how to find him?"

"I don't know where we're going," she responded. "That's up to you."

"Up to me?" I shot back. "Well, if it's up to me, we're getting the hell out of here."

The inward, unearthly look strong in her eyes, she said, "You know where we're going, you just need to relax and figure it out." She used her chin to indicate the canyon rim lying in front of us, the entrance to a slithering vortex of possibilities, virtually all of them ending badly.

"We'll stop at the edge," she said, in a tone that was certain and direct. "Then our true path will be revealed. It's in your head, I can feel it."

I kept following her, each step I made echoing the uncertainty in my heart. I was the adult here, and she was only twelve years old, but she acted much older, and her presence was formidable. Also, I thought to myself, I can "discover" that our true path is leading us the hell out of here. Then I can at least return her to the safety of civilization before I make the trek down the canyon. I might not have a choice. I have to go down, but she doesn't.

We continued on, not saying anything. The day was cool and perfect for hiking, so it didn't take too long to reach the edge of the canyon. We stopped, and I eyed the trail down. It threaded its way between two large sandstone boulders. The path was very steep, and the distance between the two rocks was so narrow a rope had been left so people could raise and lower their packs, making it easier to navigate the most difficult part of the trail. The narrow niche was taunting me, daring me to make my way through. It was as if the canyon wanted to swallow me up, and the cleft between the rocks was the mouth of a serpent, its jaws gleefully spread open, ready to devour me.

Audrey stood over the trail. I could tell she was upset, and for a moment a frail, lonely young girl who had just lost everything in the world that she knew—everything important. I felt a deep sympathy, and I struggled, wanting to help, but not knowing what to do or say. I thought about telling her everything was going to be all right, but that was a meaningless platitude. The truth was I had no idea, no real frame of reference to understand her pain. So, I stood, awkward and alone, watching her struggle.

She transformed in front of my eyes. She caught herself and straightened, "larger", though she was actually the same size. The sheer agony that had wrenched her face into a terrible grimace of desolation and loss was gone, replaced by the inwardness and a mask that displayed no emotion whatsoever. Her countenance was now a closed door that was even more heart wrenching than the pain I had seen before.

"Okay, it's time," she said in a matter-of-fact tone, as if she were commenting on the weather.

"What do you mean it's time?" I asked, a little intimidated by her.

"You need to find our way," she answered placidly.

"How am I supposed to do that?" I responded in an exasperated tone.

"Just relax and find the connection to your true self. You know what to do, you're just letting emotion cloud your senses."

I remembered the breathing exercises from my martial arts classes. These exercises allow you to find your "center" and prepare for a class, or a bout with another person. When done properly, you can feel the emotions drop away from you, and you are able to concentrate at a much higher level and get a "feel" of what is happening around you. Perhaps this would be helpful.

I closed my eyes and put my hands at my sides. I breathed, pushing down with my hands every time I exhaled. I breathed in through my nose, filling my diaphragm with air, and slowly exhaled through my mouth. This allowed me to push my emotions down, suppressing them, as I continued to breathe. I continued doing this, and as I did, I felt a great calm wave wash over me, as I found my center. I kept on, and gradually felt myself drop into a meditative state. I was aware of my surroundings, but only distantly. All physical sensations, sounds, sights, and smells faded. As in a photo washed out by the sun, the mere hints of the original contours remained.

This wasn't a usual part of my martial arts breathing, and I felt a flutter of panic at the strange feeling that came over me, but I quelled it, and continued. Disjointed images came to my mind: a mountain wreathed in cloud, and the sea, rolling waves battering the craggy rocks of a faraway beach. I heard laughter and the whisper of an all-encompassing rain. I could smell the refreshing aroma of water, and I sighed, enjoying the sensation. I felt a slight tickle on the left side of this mental image. It was light against dark, and it intrigued me. I wanted to explore this small burst of energy that lit up the night of my dream.

I tried to focus on it, to bring it closer to me, or I to it. I was unable to do so, and as I fought, trying to fathom what it was, I lost my way. The mental image slid from me, and I was back at the canyon rim and the young girl before me.

I immediately knew she was right, and I understood where we had to go. The idea of lying to her and finding an excuse to leave was gone, replaced with a sudden feeling that we needed to turn left and descend the canyon edge.

"Let's go this way," I called to her. "I think I know where we're going."

"I told you," she said calmly. "let's go."

We walked down the rim for about a half a mile. We were off the trail, and so it was a little more difficult. The earth was soft, and our feet sank into it at times. Occasionally we would cross a small sand dune, the relic of the unceasing wind and water that wore down the boulders and bluffs before the desert came and laid claim to the once verdant land. Now, out of the wind and rain, only wind remains. The sand on these dunes had small ripples, created by the wind, and the sun etched shadows in these valleys, a fine demarcation between light and dark. We pressed on and a long finger of land stretched out in front of us encroaching into the more or less uniform straight line the edge of the canyon usually presented. From the point, it was clear a vaguely triangular finger stretched out in front of us. The finger extended out into the canyon for about fifty yards, until it narrowed down to a few feet wide and ended.

We reached the final point, which created a shallow bowl in the canyon. The rim retreated in an arc to my right, and I could see the other side of the bowl scooped out of the gorge, about two hundred yards away. A small ledge underneath was about ten feet wide and followed the rough semicircle of the canyon rim, running true about thirty to fifty feet below the edge of the canyon. The ledge dropped off sharply in most places, but a rough path led from the narrow tongue down to the somewhat flat surface below. I would have to jump across a huge crack in the bluff that was about three feet wide, and then clamber down the steep face of a huge boulder, but it could be done.

I pulled out my binoculars and brought the other side of the bowl into sharp relief. I followed the ledge, which terminated on the other side of the bowl. Below the bench was an overhang, with an inset below the rich brown sandstone bluff. Excitement rose. A group of cliff dwellings nestled in the overhang, in good shape, with a couple of dwellings still sealed with rock doors. And a larger room with a rock ceiling. A square doorway was made of flat pieces of sandstone in the middle of this room. It must be a kiva. Normally I would be thrilled and would love a chance to explore and appreciate a ruin like this. Right now, though, I wasn't sure how it could help. Hand and footholds had been worn into the rock. The only way to enter the overhang from below must be up this set of steps. Countless numbers of ancient people must have used these footholds over many generations to create these impressions. Much as the wind and the rain, these people had left their indelible imprint on the very backbone of the earth.

Then a sudden realization startled me. I thought back to my dream about the ancient man securing his small village for the night. Further, I remembered the second dream, where he entered a kiva from the top and cast a spell of protection. A spell that had somehow brought Audrey back from a world that was dark, silent, and surreal. I perceived the dwellings in a whole new light: they matched the surroundings of my dream with uncanny precision. Audrey was right; I did have the answer inside me.

I handed the binoculars over to her excitedly and pointed. "A set of dwellings. I think this is what I dreamed about. I used a spell I learned from the dream to bring you back."

"Let's go," she said.

I stowed my binoculars and charted our route. I was really good at that. I jumped over to the large boulder that had cracked off the main rock formation and held out my hand to Audrey. She blithely jumped over the large gap, ignoring my hand. She was athletic and capable. I worked my way off the rock to the steep slope below. Not much room for error. The rim was only about ten feet away from the edge of the rock, and if I lost control when getting off the rock, I could end up stumbling over the edge of the precipice to the bottom of the canyon. I offered Audrey my hand again, and she took it this time.

I steadied her as she made the final descent from the rock. Then we worked our way down the steep slope to the beginning of the ledge. It was reasonably flat. I could see areas where it tightened up, and we would have to skirt the edge of the bluff to continue. I set out, maneuvering my way past dead trees and large rocks. The bench we were on held true and we made our way around the semicircle, ending up above the overhang.

We knew the dwelling was somewhere down below us: the only question was that of reaching it. A steep path led sharply down. I could see the end of the ledge the dwellings were perched on, sticking out from the side of the overhanging rock. We slowly, carefully, made our way down, and stopped about twelve feet above the small, flat area of rock that could lead us to the ancient site.

At that point I was stymied. The flat area of the bench was only about ten feet by ten feet. To our right, the rock swelled up into the overhang, with a drop of hundreds of feet to the canyon below. To the left the flat area ended in an abrupt cliff edge, also dropping straight down into the canyon far below. No sign of a trail down to the ledge. It was a sheer drop.

My eye fell on a juniper tree, about fifteen feet to my right. It was large, evidently rooted in a large depression in the overhang that had filled with dirt over the years. If I had a rope, I could probably tie it to the tree and then rappel down. It wasn't really that far, just well out of reach without some type of support. Then I found a rope I remembered from the point where the trail dropped off in the canyon: it was thick and about fifty feet long. It would be enough.

"We can make it down. All we have to do is get back to where the trail goes down in the canyon and borrow the rope for a while. We'll put it back when we're done."

Audrey was her usual loquacious self. "Let's go."

It didn't take long to get back to the trail. We were both athletic, and wasting time was pointless. I unraveled the knot on the rope and coiled it around my shoulder. It was too bulky to fit in my backpack. Then we headed back for the canyon. It was already early afternoon, and I wasn't sure what was going to happen.

We made it back to the overhang, and I looped the rope around the tree trunk, double knotting it. I took the rest of the rope and made knots in it, one about every foot. This would give me a good grip as I lowered myself down to the ledge. I put on the pair of leather gloves I always keep in my pack.

I've rappelled a few times just for fun, but this was different. For one thing I always had help and a friction device to help with lowering and climbing. This would be different, way different. For one thing, a miscalculation could result in a fall that would undoubtedly kill me. Second, I was always doing it with someone who was an experienced professional. The good news was I rappelled thirty or forty feet the other times. This time I really needed to drop and climb about ten feet. So, it was easier and harder, at the same time.

Audrey was serenely gazing out over the breadth of the canyon.

"I'll be back in a little bit," I said.

"I'll be right behind you," she shot back.

"You're not even thinking about climbing down this rope," I said, blinking in consternation.

"We already did that in gym class," she responded. "It's easy."

I mentally shrugged and shouldered my pack. It didn't weigh that much, and I wanted to have my gear with me. Then I grabbed the rope. The knots and the gloves made it pretty easy to get a good grip. I carefully situated myself so I was facing the canyon rim. Then I gingerly used my knees and feet to get an extra purchase on the rope.

Next, I slowly lowered myself down. It was slow and difficult, because the rope wasn't suspended away from the cliff face, and I was dragging against it the whole way. The knots gave me plenty of good hard projections to hang onto, and I made it down okay.

Audrey was already coming down. She was small, much lighter than I was, and she didn't have any real trouble. She continued to amaze me.

As soon as she got down, we turned and moved towards the dwelling. The rock from the overhang hid it from view. The ledge widened out as the cliff face receded, and after twenty or thirty feet we were treading comfortably on a bench that led slightly upward. The cliff dwelling came into sight about then, and we both stopped. For me it was appreciation and awe. I felt like Howard Carter, the archeologist who discovered the tomb of King Tut in Egypt.

The dwelling consisted of several rooms, all on one level. I couldn't see the top of the structures from where I stood, but I knew the large curving building on the right was the kiva. To the left were three or four other rooms: I couldn't tell from this angle. I could see the entries to each of these rooms still had the sandstone doors intact. It defied time, and even with all the other things that had happened to me lately, I was overwhelmed.

We didn't speak at all, but by some unspoken signal we both ascended the ledge, approaching the set of rooms. As we closed in, I could see a small section of the native rock still stood on the front side of the dwellings. A set of steps carved into this, which led to the roof of the structures. It was the same type of setup as the steps I'd seen with my binoculars, which must be situated somewhere below us. I climbed the steps, and the feeling of timelessness was overpowering. I thought of the man I had dreamed of, and I knew somehow that he had really existed and must have lived in this very place.

I clambered onto the roof and scrambled over the mixture of adobe and rock it was composed of. It held my weight with ease. Still strong after these many years. I moved over to the square hole in the center of the dwelling and marveled at the four large flagstones set against each other to form the entrance to the kiva. Then I bent down, trying to see inside. To my astonishment, a handmade ladder leaned against the side of hole. It must have stood in this spot for hundreds of years, patiently waiting for someone to come and make use of it once again.

I fished the flashlight out of my pack and shone it down into the kiva. It was as if I were reliving my dream. I could see the bottom of the ladder, and the piece of sandstone propped up on the other side of it, a reflector for the flames that once sprang from the fire pit. I reached down and shook the ladder gently; afraid it would fall apart.

It didn't though, in fact it held firm, a buttress against the ravages of time. I shook it harder, and then leaned in, putting some weight on the top rung. It was solid and as enduring as the stone making up the side of the canyon.

Audrey silently watched me. "I think this ladder will hold us," I said excitedly. "This is the kiva in my dream. This is where I learned the spell I used to rescue you."

I paused. She had never asked how I found her. She didn't know anything about my dream, or the spell.

Audrey came over, glanced in the hole, and then pointed down the ladder. "You'll find the answers down there," she said. "That's what we're here for."

"What are you going to do?" I asked, a little concerned.

"I'll be out here," she replied. "I'll keep an eye on things while you're napping."

Napping, I thought briefly, but then understood her reasoning. Somehow it all made sense, so I crawled down the ladder, and stepped into the kiva. I was somewhat expecting to see a treasure trove of artifacts. The room was empty though, as if the ghosts of the people who had lived here had carried off anything of importance. I swept my light over the room and noticed a small ledge protruding from the walls of the kiva, about a foot down from the ceiling. I moved the light in a circular path, following the offset in the wall as it traveled around the kiva. The shelf was remarkably empty and had almost completed a circuit of the entire room, when suddenly a figure sprang out from the darkness and into sharp relief, the light shattering the tatters of dark that had obscured it for untold years. After a small intake of breath, I went over to the shelf.

It was a carved wooden effigy, with no doubt what it represented. It was Coyote. The creator of this artifact had somehow managed to instill in the wood a sense of malice and cruelty. The carving was intricate, and the wood was finely polished juniper. The carving captured the details very well, from his canine features to the paw-hands that were a bizarre mixture of animal and human. He was standing upright of course, and as I picked up the piece and examined it, I noticed his lower legs and feet were covered with clay mixed with another substance. I didn't understand what it was all about but had a feeling the residue was somehow important.

I continued to search the kiva but didn't find anything else. I picked the north wall. I took off my pack and used it as a pillow. I got comfortable and relaxed, hoping I could go to sleep. Amazingly, I drifted off right away.

~ * ~

The ancient man, spiritual leader of his community, was frantic. Not only had Coyote taken his daughter, but now he was appearing nightly in the set of dwellings. He would come after dark and appear nightly. He would howl, laugh, and terrorize the man and any other villagers with him.

But when they tried to fight back, to hit him, use a club, or fire, he would disappear, and their attempts to defend themselves would literally fall on empty air. Ahh, but I must do something, *he thought.* Not only for my people but also for Breela. Actually, *he knew, it was mostly for Breela. He was determined to not leave her death unavenged.*

To this end, he carefully went over the songs. Could he use one to fend him off, or even better, destroy him? *He considered, and ruminated, and came up with nothing.* No songs, *the music died within him as he thought of life without his daughter. He had to take action; he just didn't know what.*

As he sat by the fire, wondering if Coyote would come this night, he had an idea. Since the song didn't exist, he must create it. *Like the growing of maize, he would start with a small kernel and slowly, patiently tend it until it flowered into a mature potent incantation, full of life, yet a bringer of death. He thought about the songs and spells he knew, and how the song and the magic intertwined with the physical to form the spell.*

Then, slowly, an idea bloomed. He created a chant, one that took its root in the earth, and crafted the words to urge earth mother to hold to that which was a part of the spell.

Then he took some adobe, that which held the walls and roofs of his home together. To this he added some corn meal, ground on the metate just yesterday. He mixed them in a bowl and mused. He would add water to them, but later. Now he needed something that would personify Coyote, unique to him. A hair or whisker would do, but how could he get one of those without leaving the tribe and going to face Coyote? He knew if he did that, then he wouldn't be coming back with a hair. Instead, Coyote would be feasting on his bones, just as he did on Breela's.

His eyes fastened on the household items that made this small circle of rock into a home. Several pots rested on the floor, along with a wooden plate and a pair of yucca sandals. A fire blazed, of course, and a bed woven of yucca fibers over a large mixture of pine needles, grass, and moss. Then of course the turkey blanket. The covering made of turkey feathers was the only one the tribe owned and his by virtue of his position. Unfortunately, he didn't see how any of these items could be of any value, at least when it came to Coyote. He glanced at the ceremonial knife; finely chipped from pure white stone, finely worked and feathered, with a wooden handle held on by piñon sap, it was beautiful and sharp, but of no value if he couldn't use it on Coyote.

He studied the wood by the fire, fuel waiting to be consumed, its potential energy unused. One large stick in particular caught his attention. It was thick and weighty, about three inches in diameter, and a foot long. It was straight and pure, not twisted or gnarled like the other pieces. He continued to gaze at it, calculating. Something was lurking, if he could just figure it out. The dimensions of the stick were about right to capture Coyote's image in a smaller form.

He reached over, picked up the stick, and remembered the words Hantu, a villager who liked to carve things in the winter, had told him, "The object you're carving is already in the wood, you just have to free it. Also, when you create an image of an animal, or a bird, you imprison a portion of the essence of the creature within. That is why my eyesight is the best of all the men in our tribe. I carved hawk and captured a part of him, which I now use to benefit both the tribe, and myself. After all, don't I share my bed with the most beautiful woman of the entire tribe?" Hantu grinned.

The shaman grabbed the ceremonial knife, pictured Coyote in his mind, and went to work, both releasing the image of Coyote, and capturing a deeper, more profound part of him at the same time.

CHAPTER 12

I woke with a start and looked around me. The dream was incomplete. I understood what this ancient man had done, but I didn't know the song he used. More importantly, I didn't know the outcome of his idea. If I bound Coyote's physical form to my apartment, or some other place, would I be able to shoot him? Could I kill him? Maybe a silver bullet? The dream had left me with more questions than answers. Either way, I had taken my "nap" as Audrey put it, and so it was time to go. I grabbed the effigy and stuck it in my pack. Then I mounted the ladder quickly and stepped out on top of the kiva.

Audrey was sitting with her back against the canyon wall, on the far side of the dwellings. She was using her pack as a pillow, just like I did.

"It's a beautiful canyon," she mused, acknowledging my presence. "Too bad it is home to such ugliness."

I glanced down the canyon. The bottom still lay a couple hundred feet below us, and so all was miniaturized by the distance from where I stood. Yet the vista was magnificent, with the red wall of the canyon across the way vivid and full of splendor in the mid-afternoon sun. From the edge of the kiva that lay next to the dwellings, it was apparent one of the rooms had fallen victim to time, and part of the wall was caved in.

On an impulse I climbed down the rock steps and approached the gaping maw that was once a finely built wall of adobe and stone. Inside a metate and mano lay patiently waiting to once again feel the warmth and familiarity of human hands. Beyond that, at the rear of the dwelling, still lying in shadow, I made out a small object. I bent over and crept into the ruin. I knelt in front of the object and recognized a corrugated pot. It was gray, with fine, regular marks indented over the entire outside surface. To my surprise, a stone lid was snugly setting atop its mouth, still guarding the contents against the weather and animals. I opened the lid out of curiosity.

It was full of small, round corn cobs. This was the maize the Anasazi used. The cobs were still full of kernels, dark red verging on purple. I marveled that the maize was still there and was probably still edible. I thought about the dream and how the man was going to use ground maize as part of the spell. I glanced over at the metate and mano and over at the wall then at the bits and pieces of adobe sticking out of the broken bulwark, mute testimony to the age of the structure and to how time had left its mark, sinking its teeth into the wall, shaking it into ragged fragments of a once perfect structure.

I immediately understood why we were here. I took the mano and awkwardly used it to break a handful of kernels out of one of the corn cobs. The rest I carefully covered with the stone lid, making sure it rested securely on the pot. I poured the corn on the metate, and carefully, reverently, used the mano to grind the corn into a coarse grain, just as the Anasazi had done hundreds of years ago. I put the grain into a zippered plastic bag. I always keep a few in my pack, as they come in handy for all sorts of things. I gathered several pieces of adobe, their edges still inscribed by the rocks that had once formed a wall. I used a regular piece of rock and gently broke the adobe into small pieces. I put a handful of these into another baggie then I went to find Audrey.

She was still sitting in the same place, as motionless and inscrutable as the Sphinx. I explained what I had found and done.

"Then we're done here," she said coolly. "Let's get out of here before He figures out we're here. We still need time to prepare."

With that, we both turned and made for the rope ladder.

It didn't take us long to get out. When you've hiked an area once and know the terrain, it goes much faster. We dropped off the rope where the trail entered the canyon and made our way to the Jeep.

CHAPTER 13

The trip back to my townhouse was unremarkable. Audrey was lost in her own world, and I was thinking about the ramifications of everything that happened in the last day. I initially set out to go ahead and go down into the canyon, even though I was terrified by what would happen to me. I felt Coyote had me trapped, and I was unable to devise a way out. The thought of a bloody pair of panties; that no doubt belonged to the woman who disappeared a couple of weeks ago—well, the thought of that being connected to me filled my stomach with ice. While I logically knew I could prove I wasn't out there at that time, I was still sickened by the thought of the press getting a hold of the story and what it could do to me. I felt it would ruin my life, even if I was never formally charged with any crime.

I marveled at how the day had progressed. I was on the way out to the canyon, wondering how to best proceed, when suddenly a flash of light, the reflection off the cell phone, a final breath of a desperate cry for aid, somehow caught my eye. Then the world suddenly transformed, and I knew more about Coyote than ever before.

And I had a partnership with a girl who showed glimpses of wisdom and knowledge that transcended any earthly explanation.

As I drove, my mind raced while I tried to put together the pieces of a puzzle named Audrey. A puzzle that was so akin to a pot dropped and shattered by one of the ancient people who had inhabited this land. The jagged remnants of her life—could they ever be put back together? If so, would they ever form a complete person, or like a broken vessel, would bitter gaps from fragments be elusive, the voids in the receptacle of her former self leaking pieces of her battered soul, just as the pot would never again hold water?

What on earth was I going to do with Audrey? Now that I was driving home, I had a chance to ponder one of the most important questions that had come from this. Now it was no longer just me against Coyote. I had another person to think about, another person I felt responsible for, and who I had a great deal of compassion for.

At the same time though, she presented a huge problem. I couldn't just show up somewhere with a twelve-year old girl who had vanished with the rest of her family a few months ago. The scrutiny would be intense and overwhelming, and the police wouldn't view any story I could conjure up favorably. Obviously, of course, I couldn't tell them the truth. That was the worst part: the truth could redeem me, even paint me in a heroic light, and yet that truth would never be held as true. It put me in a tight spot.

I decided to broach the subject with her, to find out what she wanted to do. Maybe she had some close relatives who would take her in. At least that would save her from being put into social services, and the bitter future of being an orphan—and trying somehow to find a new family.

"So, Audrey," I started hopefully. "Do you have any close relatives? Can we call someone, someone who would be willing to take you in?"

"Not really," she responded. "My mom was an only child, and my dad had one sister. I met her a couple of times, but we weren't really that close."

She glared and continued. "Anyway, Jim, right now let's not worry about that. I told you; I want Coyote's ass. I'm not going anywhere till we take care of him."

"Don't worry," she added perceptively. "I'm not going to cause you any problems."

Then her voice turned inward, and she spoke as if she were much older and weary of this world. "You're going to find other people don't really *notice* me. I know you don't quite understand what I mean right now, but you'll see."

Then she turned her head and gazed out the passenger window, effectively putting an end to our conversation.

Once again nonplused, I decided to let it go for now and continued towards home. Maybe I'd figure out what to do with her when I got there.

We pulled into the townhouse about eleven at night. I was tired, both from the drive, the hike, and all that had happened. I invited her in and asked her if she needed anything. She said no and sat down on the couch, stiffly, absorbed in her own thoughts. I fixed us both a bite to eat and as I didn't have a guest bedroom set up, I got her some blankets and a pillow for the couch. Then I gratefully fell into bed and into a deep, dreamless sleep.

I woke up the next morning feeling refreshed. I pulled my clothes on and cracked the bedroom door open, wanting to give Audrey privacy if she was still asleep. I passed by the couch and noticed the blankets were unused. She had a chair pulled up by the window and was sitting in it with her legs curled up on the seat. She faced out the window toward the encroaching dawn. The residential area where I lived had a few streetlights, casting their halos of warmth and security against the encompassing dark. In the distance the streetlights marched on towards city center, their small regular yellow circles of effulgence merging into the greater collective of brilliantly lit skyscrapers that brightened the distant horizon.

"It reminds me of when I was a little girl," she said dreamily. "I used to love the lights."

Then she came out of her reverie, visibly jerking. She spun around and stood up, facing me, a neutral expression on her face.

"Did you get any sleep last night?" I asked.

"Sleep's overrated," she responded offhandedly. "We're going to have to go back out," she said. "We need to make sure you have his attention."

"I don't really think that's such a good idea…"

"We have to make sure you have his attention," she repeated, enunciating each word slowly, as if she were speaking to a child.

"Also, we're going to need a dog collar, a piece of paper, a magic marker, and one of those plastic things you put paper in to protect it. You'd better bring your thirty-aught-six as well, with a box of ammunition."

"How do you know I've got a thirty-aught-six?" I answered, flabbergasted.

"I took a look around last night," she said. "I needed to see what you've got and what we need to buy today. We'll take off early tomorrow morning after you dream the spell."

"Dream the spell?" I asked.

"Yeah, we need to be ready for tomorrow night," she replied.

"And exactly what do you think will happen tomorrow

night?" I asked.

"He'll be coming for you," she answered.

"Okay," I said. "And what makes you think that?"

"Because you're going to send him a message. The kind of message he won't ignore. That's why we need the materials I told you about."

I shook my head in exasperation. For some reason, her blithe self-assurance was impossible to ignore. I already had the sinking feeling that it was fruitless to argue with her. Also, she was right yesterday, about finding my center and about finding the dwelling. To be brutally honest, I didn't really have any better idea about a plan of attack. So, I had my coffee, cleaned up, prepared breakfast for both of us, and then we went shopping.

The shopping trip was surreal. Audrey was right when she said people didn't really notice her. I'm not talking about people automatically deferring to me because I'm an adult and she's a child. It was completely different. Several times I observed someone notice her, and then somehow their gaze would just...slide off her, as if she were a slippery surface and their awareness just couldn't get any traction. A couple of times she slipped out of her inward self, and I noticed she was wryly amused as I watched people try to register her on a conscious level and fail, to my bemusement and amazement.

We finished shopping and went back to the house. I tried to quiz Audrey about these seemingly unconnected items I had bought, and why I needed them, but she became reticent, and just told me to wait until after the dream. Not knowing what else to do, I packed everything up and prepared to go back out. In the evening we watched an animated movie, and a couple of times she seemed normal, laughing out loud at the antics of the characters. Mostly though, she just stared through the TV screen, lost in a world of her own, the design of which was beyond my ability to understand or enter.

Thankfully, it was time to go to bed, and I lay down, praying for a restful sleep, one that would lead to the dream, and the final answer.

CHAPTER 14

The shaman sat cross legged in front of the fire. In front of him lay a rock with a wet mixture of clay and corn meal mixed together. By his side, close at hand and ready, sat the effigy of Coyote. He was humming the spell to himself, over and over. He had laid the enchantment earlier in the evening, saying the spell and adding the materials at the correct intervals. Now all he needed to do was to keep the spell active while he waited for Coyote to come.

He didn't quite understand why his spell of protection didn't work, why Coyote was able to appear in the dwelling anytime he chose, but he knew it had to do with how Coyote was visiting. Somehow Coyote was sending his spirit aloft, unfettered by physical bounds. Thus he could effortlessly cross the protective barrier the shaman had so lovingly cast. Tonight would be different though. Shaman was ready. And so were the others of his tribe. The fire was laid out on top of the kiva, and the dancing tendrils of orange and yellow would be visible from the canyon floor. His brothers and sisters, armed with clubs, bows, and knives, were strategically hidden in the shadows, waiting. They all had masks on, for in this way Coyote wouldn't know who had killed him. He wouldn't be able to haunt their essences in the afterlife if he didn't recognize his assailant. The exception to this was the shaman. He didn't care if Coyote knew him. He would be glad to thrust his ceremonial knife into the black heart of the beast and then look him in the eye as he died. His lust for revenge was such he had lost his beliefs in the afterlife anyway, which he carefully kept to himself. No need to shatter the naïve convictions of the others.

Then, in front of the fire, directly facing the shaman, an apparition came into being. Born of malevolence and power, the hated form of Coyote burst forth from angry nothingness to appear before them. He glanced around and then focused on shaman. The spiritual leader of the tribe hesitated before acting. He was trembling, a reaction born from hatred and fear, and almost lost the song he was humming. Then he caught himself, and the spell that was clothed in the verse he faithfully murmured was saved and sprang back to life.

The shaman reached down and clasped the effigy. Both Coyote and he were strangely transfixed, the intensity of their locked gazes muting the rest of the world, until Shaman and Coyote were the only particles of the universe that still existed. Shaman slowly, carefully, deliberately raised the effigy in his left hand and plunged it into the mixture of clay and cornmeal, twisting the figure back and forth as he did so, making sure the binding mixture fully adhered to the feet and legs of the wooden likeness.

"NEKRAM," he pronounced sharply, the culmination of the incantation. Coyote's eyes widened slightly, and the manifestation, although not visibly changing, somehow "felt" more solid, more real, and the shaman knew his spell had worked. He drew his knife and leapt to his feet, screaming, all the pent-up sorrow and anger over the loss of his child flaring up in an overwhelming burst of fire and emotion. He rushed Coyote, knife ready in his upraised fist, ready to pierce Coyote's body, and his soul. Coyote watched his approach and with a feline grace, adroitly slipped to the right, avoiding his rush. Then, he stuck out his leg, tripping the shaman in the process. Shaman went down hard, losing his knife and almost falling off the edge of the kiva. His sudden rush of emotion went out, like a white-hot chunk of iron dunked in a bucket of water. He slowly got up and turned to face Coyote.

Coyote bowed, both paw-hands together at his chest, a mocking parody of the greeting the cliff dwellers used to denote respect and love. Then he closed in on the shaman, slowly, deliberately cutting off his routes of escape, leaving the fall to the ledge below as his only option. The fall would only be the height of the kiva, but it would be enough to hurt or maim the shaman, especially if he fell off backwards. The shaman waited at the edge of the dwelling, keeping his eyes on Coyote and making sure Coyote's full attention was on him.

Coyote advanced slowly, silently, his whole attention on the holy man. Then, in a preternatural display of the senses, he turned to face three men who came out of the shadows. Two were armed with clubs and one with a knife. In an unspoken flash of unity, they rushed Coyote at the same time. Coyote turned and fled, easily brushing by the shaman and landing on the ledge below. Then he turned to the left and ran, heading for the end of the ledge, where the ladder was pulled up that connected the overhang with the canyon below. He flashed by the wall of the kiva and was ready to break out into the open area between the dwellings and the ladder.

Then Patu stepped from the shadows. He was easily the largest man in the tribe and known for his fierce physical strength. He bore a large heavy club, one only he could swing easily, and he used his full force to connect with Coyote as he rushed into the waiting arc of the heavy cudgel. Coyote screamed as the club made contact with his midsection, changing the arc of his flight and driving him out beyond the ledge into the waiting dark. Nothing was below him but empty space for hundreds of feet, and he screamed, a bizarre mixture of rage, fear, and unrequited love, until he crashed into the canyon floor below.

Then all was silent in the heavens and the earth as Coyote passed from space and time.

Coyote

But only for a while. Coyote could never truly be destroyed. However, Shaman intuitively understood it would be many years before Coyote could return. He knew his people would never have to worry about Coyote again, and he pondered. Perhaps it was time to leave the dwelling. The enemy was vanquished and perhaps he could find a better, easier life elsewhere. He remembered the brilliant feathers he had seen at a meeting with the other tribes a few years ago. The man who had them told him that far to the south was a land where it never snowed, and all sorts of fantastic animals and plant life thrived—even a large cat, similar to cougar, but with spots. He thought about the land that had given him and his tribe life all these years, and his heart ached at the thought of leaving. Yet he had noticed the water in the canyon was harder to find every year. Last summer the great water, a large cistern like place in the rocks that always had an ample supply of the life-giving fluid, had almost gone dry. Perhaps it was time to find a new land, one where the memories of his daughter would be far away, and he could live in peace as the thoughts of his lost child could wither and fade with time and distance. Yes, he thought, it was time to move on.

CHAPTER 15

I woke up slowly, still full of the fog obscuring the pathway between slumber and awareness. I lay in bed, unable to think about anything at all. I relived the dream, each aspect of the experience piercing me with a vibrant sense of loss and sorrow. I grabbed my phone and sang, capturing the cadence and rhythm of the shaman's chant before the memory faded, losing its color and unraveling into darkness. I finished and put the phone back down on the nightstand. The ramifications of the dream hit me. He had done it! He had used the spell of binding shackled Coyote's physical being to the spectral manifestation he enjoyed sending out to torment his beleaguered victims. That meant I too could bind him. Then I could use my pistol and send him back to whatever hell he had sprang from. I felt a dark surge of vengeful fury wash over me as I allowed a brief fantasy of retribution run its course.

Then a little nagging tendril of doubt suddenly insinuated itself into my thoughts. Like an itch between your shoulder blades, it dug in, and as I drifted into full wakefulness, I discovered a huge problem. I didn't hear the words to the incantation. My vision opened after the shaman had sung the initial spell. Without these words the whole thing was useless. Like a body without a brain, it was a shambling automaton without direction or purpose. I ran the emotional gauntlet between fierce victory and hopeless defeat in mere moments. The dark vengeance that consumed me moments ago shattering into shards of despair and desolation.

Without the entire spell I was lost. No going forward from here. I had a feeling of finality about the dream, and I somehow knew the shaman would never reach out to me again. His part in this story was over. The knowledge and experience he shared with me was meant to be sufficient. Yet it was not.

I tossed and turned for a couple of hours and got up. I opened the bedroom door. Audrey was in her usual position by the window. I knew she hadn't slept. Maybe she didn't need sleep anymore. The place she had been had changed her, taking her childish sense of wonder and perhaps her humanity. No doubt about it.

I tentatively slipped into the living room. I stood by her side. We shared the quiet joy of a warm room, with a view of the normal world outside. I understood her fascination with the city and the lights, all aspects of my life that slipped away. I wondered if I would ever be able to just go out for a cup of coffee or go to a bookstore, all the things I used to take for granted. I had a cold premonition Coyote was going to win this one. That's what happens when you take on a creature older than the world and imbued with mysterious power.

I cleared my throat, searching for the words to explain to Audrey I had failed. There was no other way than head on. No use circling around the subject.

"I had a dream again last night. I saw Coyote and the shaman. Coyote was visiting the shaman every night, and he could see him, but he couldn't touch him. Somehow, he just disappears when you try to attack him. The shaman used the effigy I found and cast a spell of binding to somehow make Coyote's apparition physical. They fought him and won. A big guy knocked him off the cliff and he fell into the canyon, screaming all the way. I loved it."

Audrey gave me a sideways glance, her inward gaze only briefly focusing on me. She didn't speak, but her silence somehow indicated understanding and encouraged me to continue.

"There's a big problem. I didn't dream true. My vision started after the shaman sang the incantation he used to bind Coyote. I know the tune, but I don't know the words. Without words the song is useless. I'm sorry, but I don't know what else to do."

Audrey froze in place. She smiled, an expression full of other-worldly compassion and understanding. "It's okay," she said softly. "The words will come to you when you really need them. Now it's time to go. We need to send Coyote a message."

"Go where?" I asked. "Don't you understand?" I continued, irritated by her continued unruffled demeanor. "I didn't get the words. They're not here." I knocked my forehead with open palm. "I don't have them, and I know the shaman isn't coming back. The dreams are over. We're finished. We can't fight a monster we can't hit." I squeezed my temples with both hands, trying to calm down, trying to make her understand.

"We have to send Coyote a message," Audrey replied, ignoring my comments. "We need to draw him out. You see, he doesn't know something."

"And what would that be?" I responded testily.

"Me," she said calmly. "He can't see me. He thinks I'm gone," she continued, staring through me, staring at forever. "But he's wrong. I'm still here. For now."

"What difference will that make?" I asked, intrigued despite myself.

"It will make all the difference," she answered calmly. "He won't see what's coming. He can't, because it's hidden from him."

"Okay," I said. "So, what is it that you are going to do? How are you going to make a difference?"

"I can't tell you," she replied.

"Why not?" I said, exasperated with her obliqueness.

"Because it would give you hope," she said. "Coyote would pick up on it and be a little more careful. I want him to see your fear and despair. We need for him to be sure of himself. We need for him to give me some time."

I considered. I wanted to believe, because belief would give me the hope she talked about. She met my gaze evenly, indifferently. In her eyes blazed the fire of a thousand suns. I had no other choice. I had to roll with it, with no other viable option. The vision of a pair of bloody panties dangling from his paw-hand was always in the back of my mind, a cold heavy stone in the pit of my stomach. It was either this or go confront Coyote down in the canyon by myself. I couldn't afford to ignore him. That would end in disaster for sure. So I gave up and turned to the kitchen. I would need coffee, and we both would need breakfast before I left.

CHAPTER 16

This time I came in on the back road. This was the path that led me to my initial confrontation with Coyote. It was on the other side of the canyon from the trailhead and quite a distance up the canyon. I had the rifle, my binoculars, and the dog collar, along with the Magic Marker and the plastic sheet. I pulled up at the end of the road, the juniper tree where Coyote had merged with the shadow casting reflections of memory as I parked the Jeep and readied the stuff.

Audrey wasn't with me for this one. Based on her idea, that she was hidden from Coyote, we decided to make sure she stayed that way. I headed over to the canyon rim and shouldered the rifle. I fired down into the gorge, not trying for any particular target. This wasn't about hitting anything. I was just trying to get something's attention. I fired twice more, for a total of three shots spaced five seconds apart. The international call for distress is three of anything, a flash of light or whistle blast, with a five second interval. The canyon was lonely and remote, and I knew the shots wouldn't attract the attention of any other people. On the other hand, a certain creature that was something other than human might find the shots an irresistible opportunity to have some fun. At least that was the idea.

I settled in to wait, the rifle re-loaded, and I used my binoculars to carefully scan the landscape about me for any sign of movement. I used the field glasses intermittently, trying to ensure I would spot any sign of unusual activity around me before it was too late.

Ten minutes later I spotted a flash of gray about two hundred yards down the canyon rim, a flicker that appeared between the trunks of two trees and then disappeared back into the cover of the surrounding undergrowth. I cautiously raised my rifle and peered through the scope. I slowly scanned the surrounding sage brush and mix of juniper and piñon trees, hoping to home in on the movement, transforming the twinkle of color into a more substantial manifestation of the creature that had caused it.

I continued searching, the trees and brush contrasting sharply with the reddish-brown soil and the interplay of shadow and sun sprinkled the terrain with rich tones of light and dark brown. I didn't see anything for a bit, but then a coyote sauntered slowly out into an opening between a clump of sagebrush and a tree, about one hundred yards away. The beast stood with no apparent sign of fear or discomfort. Then it leapt to its hind legs and gave two short, sharp barks, returning to all fours after. I heard a distant bark in response and knew I didn't have much time. I was getting their attention.

I picked up the rifle and aimed at the coyote. He was just standing watching me. I squeezed the trigger and took him out, a clean shot to the heart. No use in an animal needlessly suffering. Then I ran over, carrying the stuff with me. I slipped the dog collar around its neck and attached the plastic sleeve to the collar. The paper was already inside the protective cover. On it I had written, in big, bold letters:

YOU'RE NEXT MOTHER FUCKER.

I dragged the coyote to the canyon rim. It was one of the places with a sheer drop of fifty feet or so. I grabbed the collar and slung the coyote over into the canyon. Then I ran back to the Jeep.

I got to the car, started it, and turned around quickly. Then I lit out as quickly as the rough road would allow me to drive without risking both myself and the vehicle. I figured I had Coyote's attention now. I just wasn't sure what I was going to do with it. I reached the top of a small hill the road bisected on its way from the rim. I topped over and noticed the trees on my right were wildly waving, the branches writhing as if they were in pain. I was at a loss. I didn't understand what was happening. Then, as I thought back to my initial conversation with Audrey, I realized with a sick horror this must be the phenomenon she had described. So, Coyote was right here, right now.

I gave the Jeep more gas, and I could hear the engine rpms saw back and forth as the Jeep clawed its way across the rough terrain, sometimes digging in, and other times catching air from the rough ride. I clenched my hands on the steering wheel, desperately striving to keep my grip. I couldn't afford to lose control of the Jeep.

Coyote

The phenomenon raced through the trees, making an intercept course with the road. I could see it picking up speed, one tree after another possessed by insanity, turning into a gibbering mass of branches. The Jeep bucked and skidded and then bounced over a last patch of rocky ground and onto one of the strangely smooth spots you occasionally find on these off-road paths. I jammed the gas all the way to the floor, and the Jeep responded instantly, like a wild horse suddenly freed from its reins. I blasted down the road, throwing a huge plume of dust. The trees directly in front of me squirmed, as if they had ants in their pants. The anomaly had arrived at the road. I took a breath, clenched my teeth, narrowed my eyes to mere slits, and hit the phenomenon full force.

I had a brief sensation of unremitting, all-encompassing pain. My entire body felt as if it were being sliced apart by razors, especially my head and my eyes. My vision grew dim, and the road in front of me filled with black spots. I desperately fought with the darkness that relentlessly threatened to overcome my will but managed to keep the Jeep straight somehow, and then I was blissfully, mercifully through the barrier and onto the regular terrain on the other side. I gasped and instinctively slowed down. In the mirror behind me, all I could see was a billowing cloud of brown dust.

After the painful sensations faded away, I was half expecting to find blood gushing out in a hundred different places. There was no sign of damage. Just like Audrey said, it cut without cutting, hurt without hurting. The Jeep didn't care one way or the other. It ran like always, as smooth as silk. I shook, a reaction to the close call I had just experienced. I knew when I got a little farther down the road I would stop for a minute and get my bearings, but not until I was far away from the phenomenon and Coyote. One thing for sure, if Audrey wanted to guarantee he would be paying us a visit, she was going to get her wish.

I headed back for the house, driving as fast as I could. I wanted to get to my destination before dark. I definitely didn't want to leave Audrey alone, with Coyote on the rampage. I drove along, one part of my mind on the road, the other running non-stop, on a loop playing out the possible endings to this scenario. I knew Coyote would come tonight. I also knew he wouldn't hesitate to follow through on his threat to me. If I didn't figure out some way to invoke the spell, I would have to bite the bullet and go back to the canyon.

I thought about possible ways to find him. I could buy camouflage and sneak into the canyon with my rifle. I could try to find a place above the point where I originally saw him overseeing the strange ritual. Then I could wait and see, maybe they congregate regularly. Maybe I could just sit tight until midnight and he would appear, like a lamb to the slaughter, waiting for me to shoot him.

Maybe…maybe…maybe…too many maybe's.

Then my mind shifted, and I thought about particulars. Actually, what do I know about casting spells? Nothing, I just repeated what I had seen in a vision, and it worked. I didn't know why it worked, or how each part of the incantation fit with the surrounding pieces. A germ of an idea took root in my mind and grew, bearing the fruit of a full-blown alternative as I examined it from different angles.

Let's start with the basics. What is a spell? Pure and simple, it's magic. It's the stuff of books and movies. It's for fun, and entertainment, nothing more. And yet there I was, an IT guy, someone who was firmly grounded in technology, using a spell to return a young girl to this world and now trying to find the right incantation to defeat a god. A spell—it has power, and once invoked, it becomes more than the sum of its parts, and it takes on a life of its own. No science (that I know of) can explain the workings of a spell. So, I needed to throw my troubleshooting and technical skills out the window and had to think in a new way.

I considered this, and at the same time I thought about my initial confrontation with Coyote, the time in the parking garage. What had he said, why was he so offended and angry? "You weren't meant to see that. It is for us, not you. Humans aren't allowed, aren't supposed to know." Maybe something could help.

Then I had a flash of insight of what might achieve my goal. The coyotes were singing, carrying a definable tune, down in the canyon. It bore an uncanny resemblance to "Figaro," but with some subtle changes in style and cadence. Could I use this for my spell? I considered the possibility. Everything else came from a different time and a different place in this world. I had an effigy of Coyote carved hundreds of years ago, and corn that had survived, sealed in a pot, for just as long. The adobe was the glue that made it possible for the Anasazi to make remote canyons and forbidding cliffs their home.

This ritual I had stumbled onto, how old was it? I was willing to bet even older than the cliff dwellings. The mournful refrain they had created was truly a part of the very essence of Coyote. I didn't know if it would work or not, but hope was reborn, my mind full of excitement as a possible answer finally emerged. I eased my phone out of its holster and scrolled through the files, until I located the audio I had recorded that night. I hadn't really thought about it since then, because my life had taken a turn in a totally unforeseen direction, and so it would be my first time to listen to it.

I selected the file and waited impatiently for it to start playing. I eased the volume up and listened. The harmonizing of the throats of dozens of coyotes permeated the cabin of the Jeep, creating an atmosphere laden with an otherworldly, sinister ululation. The phone had captured the sound of their unearthly music perfectly, and even the recording gave me chills, the skin on my arms crawling with goose bumps as the inhuman melody cycled towards an unbearable crescendo.

That did it. I was satisfied. I was going to create a spell, and modern technology was going to help me do it.

CHAPTER 17

I parked the Jeep in the garage and hurried into the townhouse. It was getting close to dark, and I had noticed Coyote always visited me after the sun set. I had a feeling he wasn't going to wait very long tonight, and so I needed to get busy. I rushed into the living room. Audrey sat on the couch, hands in her lap, head slightly lowered. She was gazing off into space, dwelling in a world that was beyond the ken of the rest of humanity. She snapped out of it as I sat down on the other end of the couch, and glanced at me, the question in her eyes.

"I sent him the message," I said. "And I'm positive he got it."

I continued, recounting what I had done and how I had experienced a very close call with Coyote.

"Good," she stated flatly. "That means he'll be here soon. You need to get ready."

I nodded, already preoccupied with my next task. I turned into the kitchen and went through the shelves. I needed a place to mix the clay and corn. My plastic containers felt wrong. I had a couple of metal pans, but they weren't right, either. Then my eyes strayed over to a wooden tray I had. I used it to set on my lap while watching TV. It was the perfect size to hold a plate of food and a soda, or coffee. It was manmade, of course, but it was wood, not some artificial material. I had a feeling it would work.

I grabbed the two bags, one containing corn meal, the other pieces of adobe from the ruin. I found a pestle I occasionally used and broke up the bits of clay into finer particles. Then I carefully mixed the corn meal and clay together. I got a cup of water from the sink and poured a little bit of it into the mixture. I wanted it to be wet, but not soupy. It needed to be sticky, so the spell would reflect this onto Coyote, when I stuck the effigy into the mixture. I continued adding water in sparing amounts, using a wooden spoon I had to combine the ingredients. When I was satisfied, I took the whole thing over to my easy chair in the corner of the living room, across from the kitchen. This way Coyote would have his back turned to Audrey, as we faced off.

Coyote

I didn't know what her part in this was going to be. I only knew what she told me, she was invisible to him and he wouldn't see her coming. The other part, where she wanted Coyote to see me afraid and full of doubt, wasn't going to be a problem.

I took the pistol and placed it on the arm of the chair. I had a small towel which I placed on my lap, with the wooden tray over it. I kept the effigy hidden under the edge of the towel. I began with the same deep breathing exercises I used to find the dwelling. I knew I would have to be centered for this to work. In through the nose, out through the mouth, filling my lungs with air each time. Thus, I expelled the negative emotions and allowed the troubled currents of my soul to lapse into a calm body of water, unruffled by any breeze and reflecting perfectly the harmony of mind and spirit.

I reached over slowly, carefully, and clicked on the audio file of the coyotes singing. The haunting melody filled the living room and sank into the waters of my meditative state, creating a small ripple, which briefly coursed across the surface, threatening to break the trance like state I had achieved. A part of me that was far away reached out and calmed the waters, and the ripple faded away into the far reaches of the universe. The song of the coyotes rose and fell, and I hummed, lightly and then stronger with more confidence, a counterpoint to their eerie refrain. Slowly but surely, my tune intertwined and harmonized with the other, creating a new, more vibrant song.

Then I reached over, still humming, and reduced the volume on the phone. Cautiously I worked, making sure the beating heart of the binding incantation accepted its new home, and seamlessly transferred its power to the voiceless tune the shaman had used. Sensing the spell was safely transferred, I put the phone down, allowing the music from the file to run to its end. Then I continued humming and waited.

Audrey sat on the kitchen floor, cross legged, patiently waiting. I could tell she knew Coyote would come and she needed to be ready. It seemed as if she were keeping a part of herself focused on this world, waiting for the sign Coyote was here, and the rest she kept still, saving her energy for the battle to come.

CHAPTER 18

Coyote furiously paced the cave, waiting. He knew his power was greater at night; that was why he always waited till dark to send a part of himself far from the cave. How dare this pathetic human intrude into his territory and kill one of his own. He would make him pay. Tonight he would come and make sure this *Jim* knew the consequences of his actions. This human would return to the canyon and the fate that awaited him, or he would expend every effort to ruin his life. After all, several trophies of his last two hunts were displayed in the cave, and he had enough knowledge of the outside world to make sure law enforcement would get incontrovertible evidence of this human's involvement in the disappearance of the people out in canyon country. Yes, he was going to enjoy tonight's visit.

CHAPTER 19

I sat in the chair, humming. Have you ever noticed humming is a useful mechanism to improve concentration; that it can allow a person to maintain focus for long periods of time? I used this to relax and yet maintain awareness, all at the same time, like a cat waiting to pounce, muscles totally at rest and yet ready to burst into action. My awareness of the surroundings flickered as I continued maintaining a trance like state. I wished he would come, and then at least it would be over. Waiting was the hardest part.

And suddenly he was standing in front of me. I startled slightly and then caught myself. I couldn't afford to lose focus now. I flicked the cover off the effigy. Coyote's eyes widened as he recognized what I had. A glimmer of doubt crossed his canine features, probably as he remembered what had happened the last time he had seen this figure.

I grabbed the effigy and spoke the word of power I remembered from the vision.

"NEKRAM," I screamed, and plunged the effigy into the mixture of meal and clay.

Coyote somehow brightened and became more…definite. I knew the spell had worked, and I picked up the pistol, and trained it on him.

Coyote bowed, sweeping off his hat. "Well done, Jim," he drawled sardonically. "I don't know how you found the effigy or how you figured any of this out, but well done indeed."

I stared at him, a mixture of fury and fear roiling in my stomach. I knew what I had to do. Audrey had told me to keep his attention as long as possible. I didn't know what she had planned, but I knew she needed time. I was doing my part and giving it to her.

"I found the cliff dwelling," I said slowly. "And the shaman, he came to me in my dreams. That's how I found the effigy. He showed me the effigy, and he taught me how to bind you into a physical form."

"The shaman," Coyote hissed contemptuously. "I took the shaman's daughter and fed on her bones."

"I know," I replied. "But you also fell screaming to your death, now didn't you?"

"I did?" he said sarcastically. Then he grinned at me. "If I died then why am I here right now?"

"I don't know," I admitted. "But what I do know is he got rid of you, at least for a while." Then I raised the pistol slightly and aligned the sights on his head. I trembled slightly, both with fatigue from holding the pistol and desire to pull the trigger.

Then I noticed Audrey out of the corner of my eye. She was standing in the kitchen, with her arms held above her head. She was swaying slightly, and I didn't know what she was doing.

"Do you really think you can kill me with that thing?" Coyote sneered. "Maybe I'll just reach out and take it from you."

Then he laughed, and one of his arms paw-hands shot out towards me, quicker than the eye could see. I flinched despite myself, and he tossed his head back laughing.

My palms sweated, my fear overcoming me. I wasn't sure if I could hit him if he came for me, as he was fast, and if I did, whether it would do any good. I hoped Audrey would hurry up.

Then I noticed a few black tendrils rising up out of the carpet in my living room. Like cobras rising to the flute of a snake singer, they danced swayed as they formed a semicircle around Coyote's back and sides. They continued to grow getting thicker and rising up to his shoulders. They multiplied, caging him, blocking his way

"I don't know if I can kill you," I shot back, "but I bet it'll hurt like hell." I kept the gun trained on him, ready to shoot if I had to.

I didn't want to fire. I didn't know how it would play out, even if I hit him. Second, Audrey had given me specific instructions not to shoot unless absolutely necessary. I hoped these tendrils were going to work.

Coyote grinned at me, then he broke in. "The police are going to be really interested in your closet. How are you going to explain all the stuff that belonged to the people that disappeared? I've read about your prisons. You'd be a juicy little bit of young stuff, now wouldn't you?"

The thought of going to prison paralyzed me, but I just needed to keep his attention focused on me, one hundred percent, for a little while longer. The strange, ropy tentacles continued growing; now forming a thick impenetrable mass around Coyote's back and sides. I just didn't see how she was going to bring these dark, fibrous arms around the rest of him without gaining his attention.

"I've got my rifle, the one I killed your brother with. Maybe I'll sneak down in the canyon and wait for you. Then I'll just pick you off, and you'll never see it coming."

Coyote scoffed. "Do you really think you can just go down in that canyon and find me? You got lucky, once, and stumbled on me the one day a year I'm vulnerable. The rest of the time…" he trailed off expressively.

"I guess I made it down into "your" canyon and found the cliff dwelling, and you had no idea," I retorted.

I noticed the tendrils were getting thicker at Coyote's sides, and Audrey tensed up.

Coyote, clearly troubled, hesitated. I knew I'd scored a point. He wasn't sure how I'd managed to find the cliff dwelling, and he wasn't sure how he had failed to notice me.

Then Audrey attacked, a beautiful, wrathful moment. She slowly, smoothly pushed her arms forward, a dreamy, underwater motion as if against resistance. In one concerted motion, the mass of tentacles at his side moved smoothly, swiftly forward, enveloping Coyote in a cage of dark, writhing tendrils. The ends of the tentacles from both sides interlaced with each other, and I could see new shoots of growth coming up from the floor in front of him.

Coyote froze, and I could see in his eyes new emotions, ones he hadn't experienced for thousands, maybe tens of thousands, of years. I saw fear, indecision, and a sense of impending doom, all feelings he loved to feed upon from his hapless victims, yet little known to him.

I got the feeling he didn't like these new emotions.

He whirled around in place, trapped by the tentacles. He was facing Audrey now, and even though I couldn't see his expression, I could see the shock go through him in a wave as he realized who, and what, she was.

"You," he breathed. "Oh, very well done, Jimmy boy, very well done indeed. I'll give you this much, you have made this game much more interesting than I ever thought possible."

Then, with a roar, he attacked the tendrils in front of him, screaming a scarlet inundation of rage and pain.

The tentacles were strong, and I knew Audrey had somehow brought them from the place she had been. They were a manifestation of the same power Coyote used. But Coyote was not a man: he was a god, outside of time and space, and he used all his power against them. Screaming with rage and force, he clawed at the thick, ropy growth, and blood sprayed across my carpet, whether his or the phenomenon, or both, I couldn't say. Bits and pieces of the dark rope-like material filled the air as Coyote ripped and sawed, and the sound of his claws biting into the tendrils was a rending, visceral, ragged shriek, much like the splintering of wood or bone. Blood exploded into the air, blossoming into a penumbra of brilliant, metallic mist. It hovered, birdlike, and then floated to the floor.

Audrey was failing. She was pushing with all her might, but sweat was running from her face, and she was trembling with exhaustion and pent-up rage.

Coyote continued, roaring and breaking, battering the wall in front of him. I was afraid I was going to have to shoot him, and I raised the pistol.

"No," Audrey screamed.

Then, with a final push that ravaged the extremity of her will and emotion, Audrey closed the opening Coyote had made in his fibrous prison. Slowly but surely, the black walls pressed into Coyote, moving closer together.

"No," Coyote howled, and this time I heard a wonderful torrent of pure terror in his voice.

I could still see his face, and he searched frantically about for a way out.

Then the tentacles closed around his face as well, and he was gone, smothered in the tentacles. Audrey closed both of her fists, and the mass retreated inwards on itself, growing smaller and smaller, taking Coyote with it as it diminished. It kind of slid out of this world and into another, giving the unsettling impression as it departed of leaving at an angle.

It was over. Coyote was gone, not killed, but instead trapped on a world of darkness, with smooth glass buildings and silence. I thought it a fitting resting place for the monster that had very nearly ruined my life, and had destroyed Audrey, and had spread sorrow and despair over thousands of years on this earth.

CHAPTER 20

The big question now, of course, was where do we go from here? I sat the gun down and slumped over. I was covered in sweat and wracked with nervous exhaustion, both from the strain of the spellcasting and the adrenalin rush of having Coyote in front of me, a wrathful god seeking to devour those who opposed him. I glanced into the kitchen and didn't see Audrey. I gathered myself up and forced my way into the kitchen, fighting the overwhelming exhaustion that threatened to overcome me.

Audrey was lying on the floor. She was pale and cool to the touch. I felt for a pulse in her wrist but couldn't find any. I panicked as I searched for vital signs. Then I found a brief fluttering pulse, weakly sending out a mute vibration, the trembling thread of a spider's web gently pulsating to a delicate touch. I gasped with relief and got ready to pick her up and take her out to the Jeep. The emergency room was only ten minutes away, and I didn't want to wait for the ambulance to arrive.

Then she moaned, and her eyes fluttered open, her gaze not inward, but otherworldly, similarly to people captured in photos at their last minutes on earth. "Don't take me to the hospital," she rasped. "They won't see me, can't help me. It's Coyote—he grabbed a piece of me as I threw him out. Now we're connected, and he's pulling me into that world. When he pulls enough of me, I'll die."

Then I understood. Her life was like a seam, holding the two parts together, body and soul.

Coyote was slowly pulling her soul into the other world, and Audrey was becoming unraveled, stitch by stitch. I had to figure out a plan, or both parts of her would be lost forever.

CHAPTER 21

Then I had an idea. I couldn't help it. It crept into my head like a spider. It was the kind of idea that makes you furtively turn around, to see if anyone notices, even though it's only a thought.

Audrey is going to die anyway, so why not let her go. She's the one who is tied to Coyote, not me. I'll be rid of him and able to live my life, regardless of whether I help Audrey or not.

I didn't know how to help her anyway. What could I do to somehow sever a "psychic" thread between a child who is half of this world, half of another, and some bizarre animal god? *Sure, maybe I should be a good team player and put all my energy into helping Audrey. Maybe I should even give my life, if necessary. But I ponder my life and the rest of society, and I have a simple question, why?*

I knew the truth. If she was twenty-two instead of twelve, she wouldn't give me the time of day. She would be like all the rest of the girls I've met, either nice but putting me firmly into the "friend" category, or actually allowing her disdain to show on her face when she even notices me. I felt my lips tighten as I thought back to my social life, or lack thereof, and how I had been treated by women over the years. I purposefully allowed myself to open a door I usually kept firmly shut and thought back to my last date. It had been with a young lady named Ann, and it ended in a way that increased my bitterness and distrust of women.

It was a typical example of one of my hapless attempts at dating, and it was very useful to me right now. I wanted to harden my heart against Audrey. Not the person she was right now but the person she would become, one of those who think they are better than me. One of those who shut me out and left me alone, suffering with eternal loneliness and a feeling of inadequacy. I wallowed in this sensation for a while, getting in real deep, and then I felt my lip curl a bit, my mind made up, and went out to the Jeep.

I took a blanket and a pillow and arranged the back so she would be comfortable on the ride out. I may be willing to walk away from her and refuse to risk myself to help her, but I had no desire to deliberately hurt her. I just wanted to be out of this situation.

I went back inside, carefully picked her up, and carried her out to the Jeep. She moaned a couple of times as I made my way out, but she never really came to. She was definitely out of it, in really bad shape. A part of me really felt sorry for her, and I felt my resolve waiver as I got ready to close the back hatch on the Jeep. Was this really what I wanted to do? I chewed my lip. I stopped before it bled. I felt a light sheen of sweat cover my face, the guilt of what I was doing effervescing off my soul and onto my skin. A curtain of darkness flashed in my head, and I shut the back of the Jeep. It was time to go.

The drive out to desert country was quiet, surreal. Audrey was in the back, and the only indication she was even in the car was an occasional low moan, almost unheard above the road noise created by the Jeep. I was distracted and having a hard time keeping my mind locked in on driving. I almost caused an accident at one intersection when I pulled out in front of a car, the blast of the horn and squeal of brakes jolting me back into the here and now.

Audrey was haunting me. My mind kept flashing to our different times together and how she was so "otherworldly" and yet showed extreme vulnerability and pain. Leaving her to die was going to be very difficult, I rationalized, but necessary. I decided it was okay to feel remorse and guilt for what I was doing. Really, no other choice existed. I couldn't just abandon her in my apartment to die, and I couldn't help her, I didn't even know how. Yes, no doubt about it. I was doing the best thing under the circumstances.

Hours later, I arrived at the trailhead. Even though only a couple of days had passed since my last visit, it seemed like a life-time ago. I opened the back of the Jeep and carefully lifted Audrey out. She was so light, so frail, in my arms. The Jeep was the only vehicle at the parking lot, so I didn't need to worry about running into anyone. I already knew from experience they wouldn't notice Audrey anyway, she was too much a part of another world to be recognized as a part of this one. I adjusted her as best I could and headed down the trail.

It was a difficult hike. I'd never carried anything in my arms for a mile before, only on my back. I had to stop and rest a few times, and my arms were quivering with exhaustion when I spotted the little raised area of ground where I had originally found her. I hiked over, making sure to exit the trail in a rocky area where I wouldn't leave footprints, and found the place where she had existed in some sort of stasis the whole winter. I wasn't sure why I wanted to put her back exactly where I found her, but it just seemed right. I laid her down and put her small pack beside her. My feet somehow wouldn't go.

She was still out of it, and she just lay on the ground, ashen face as if she were a ghost already. I found control of my legs, and I slowly turned and headed back for the trial.

I made my way through the trees and small clumps of sagebrush for about fifty feet, circling around a cactus that lay in wait, ready gleefully sink its spines into an unwary traveler. I trod down the gentle passage that marked the transition between the uplift and the area around the trail.

Suddenly the ground in front of me erupted. A terrible, rending scream accompanied dirt and rocks shooting from the ground and into the air, creating a cloud of dust and particles, an explosion of darkness and rage, and unremitting sorrow.

I freaked out and ducked, not sure what was going on. I tried to figure out what had caused the explosion. Was someone shooting at me?

An apparition manifested in front of me. A translucent pale white thing hung in the air. It was made up of several layers, the palest white interspersed with nothing. I had seen this thing once before! When I had cast my original spell and had brought Audrey back into this world, a presence had sprung up from the ground and hovered around while I finished the incantation. I remembered that Audrey said Mommy was present and she helped me. I realized with a sharp visceral horror this was Audrey's mom.

I took off running in a blind panic, desperate to get back to the Jeep, to get away from this presence. Audrey's mom and my feelings of guilt and cowardice all propelled me towards the parking lot, working in unison to drive me forward despite my exhaustion. As I gained the trail and turned toward the trailhead another explosion happened, off to my right, accompanied by a savage, rasping scream of despair. I continued to run, willing the distance to the Jeep to narrow. The trees and rocks flashed by on the side of the trail, and soon I could see the parking area stretched out in the distance in front of me.

I slowed as I approached the trailhead. I was dead tired, my breath coming in deep labored gasps, and I bent over, my hands on my knees, resting. A few beads of sweat rolled down my forehead and into my eyes, and I wiped the droplets off with my hand, clearing the stinging from my eyes.

I walked towards the Jeep, the familiar chirping as the doors unlocked a welcome sound, a signal that this experience was almost over. The welcoming sound of gravel crunched under my feet, music to my ears.

The ground exploded again, this time directly in front of me. Gravel showered my car, little pinging sounds as rock impacted metal. The apparition was in front of me, blocking my entry to the car. Then the same savage scream ululated through the parking lot. The rasp of two pieces of metal forced to grind against each other, a harbinger of pain and loss. The specter didn't really seem aware of me, didn't have any ability to directly interact with me, and so I carefully skirted around it and headed for the car. As I reached out to open the door a brief cry rang out. Mournful and low, redolent with suffering and despair, the sound filled the air and withered away, the last breath of sunlight carried away on the wings of the night.

The utter loss and finality of this cry pierced me, slicing through my conscience. The apparition disappeared. I could *feel* the emptiness around me. Audrey's mother had given up and was no longer here. I was free to head home: no more barriers.

The drive home was uneventful. I was tired and couldn't wait. I decided to stop at the supermarket on the way at a nice one a few miles from my place. I went in and headed over to the produce department. I was checking out the apples, trying to decide which was better, when I felt a tug on my shirt. I saw a little girl about five years old. She had blonde hair and blue eyes, and was wearing a pair of jeans with a plain pink t-shirt.

"I can't find my mommy," she said plaintively.

Four or five women were scattered about the aisle.

"So, none of those are your mom?" I inquired, sweeping my hand in their general direction.

She shook her head resolutely.

No store employees were visible. I had an idea. I would just take her to customer service.

"Let's go that way," I said, pointing toward the front of the store. "We'll find someone to help you."

She nodded okay, and we walked to the front of the store. On the way I thought, *if her mom sees me with her daughter, she might think I'm trying to kidnap her. Why did she have to pick me to ask for help, with all those women all over the place?* I felt like a set of crosshairs were centered on my back as I made my way up to the front of the store, the little girl in tow.

I got a bit nervous and couldn't wait to get her to customer service, to get rid of her. We rounded the end of the aisle and headed over towards the counter, the placid little girl beside me. As I approached the counter a woman suddenly appeared from another aisle.

"*There* you are," she said, "I've been looking all over the place for you."

"I got lost," the little girl said, somewhat shamefacedly. Then she ran over and hugged her mom, grabbing her by the legs. Her mom bent over and hugged her back. Then she stood and turned toward me.

"Thanks so much for taking care of her," she said. "I really appreciate it."

"Oh, it was no big deal," I replied, a bit awkwardly. "I was glad to help."

Then, feeling a bit defensive, I continued, "I don't know why she asked me for help—lots of women around she could have asked."

"Oh, I'm not surprised," her mom replied. "Children have a good sense about these things. They know a nice person when they see them."

"Yeah, I guess," I said. "Well, see you later."

"Bye," the little girl said and smiled at me, waving.

"Bye," I responded and waved back. She was cute, and I liked her.

Then I went back to shopping, heading back to figure out which type of apple to pick. I stood reading the different descriptions, but my mind kept going back to the little girl and her mother. I was worried that if she saw me alone with the little girl, she might think I was trying to take her, but instead she seemed very happy the girl had chosen me to ask for help. I thought about Audrey, and I had to wonder why that little girl had chosen me to ask for help.

I arrived at the house and unpacked my groceries. The place gave the sensation of being off, empty. I cooked dinner, still mulling over what was wrong, what was out of place. I grabbed a couple of plates out of the cupboard without really thinking and put them on the table. Then I went over and opened the drawer for the utensils. Suddenly I stopped. Why was I setting a place for two when it was just me? Then it dawned on me. Even though she had only been with me a short time, I had become used to Audrey's presence. That's why the place felt empty.

I frowned as I put the extra one back and tried to occupy my thoughts with cooking. I just wanted to get Audrey out of my head, to stop thinking about her. Somehow, though, no matter what I did, she kept pushing her way into my thoughts, like a bulldozer, she tenaciously battered her way through my defenses.

I finished dinner and went into the living room. I decided to watch a movie until a little later, when I could go to bed. I was enjoying the thought of getting some sleep. The movie dragged on, and I tried to get interested in it, but my mind kept wandering. Even though it was still a little early, I gave up and went to bed. At least I wouldn't have to worry about waking up and finding Coyote in my room.

~ * ~

It was a warm summer's day in the forest, and a small creek meandered through the trees in front of me. The sun was shining through the trees, shafts of yellow light interspersed with shade cast by the trees. The ground was covered with grass and pine needles, and it was springy to the touch as I wandered slowly, getting closer and closer to the stream. Then I noticed a person on the other side of the stream. It was a woman, and she was off to my right but walking at such a rapid pace she would soon catch up with me and then pass me by. She had dark hair, and it hung down, obscuring her face. I noticed as she came closer her face was turned away from me.

She continued on, silently approaching. I felt a sudden pain in my chest, some sort of longing. It was my mother! My mom, how I missed her! She had died when I was young, and I was bereft, cut off from all compassion and understanding. I wanted to see her, to talk to her, and I called out as she neared.

"Mom, is that you? What's going on, where are you going?"

She ignored me and continued down the other side of the stream, her face still turned away from me.

"Why won't you look at me?" I cried. "Please, what's wrong, what did I do?"

She didn't answer and actually picked up her pace a bit. Now she was in front of me and drawing slowly away. I knew if I didn't take action, she would soon pass out of my sight.

I picked up my pace and ran, trying as hard as I could to close the gap, to get closer to her. It didn't do any good: no matter how hard I tried, no matter how fast I ran, she kept getting farther and farther away.

"Mom, no," I screamed. "Just wait a minute, I can explain. Please come back," I called plaintively.

Then the creek turned, and as it did my mother began to disappear, her silhouette lost occasionally in the trees, but then becoming more and more distant, until I could only glimpse mere flashes of her.

~ * ~

Then she was gone, and only the forest remained. Anguish seared my soul, and when oblivion crashed itself around me, I woke up.

It was 2:43 a.m. I was wide awake; the dream with my mother had shaken me. Have you ever had a dream that felt so real it was indistinguishable from reality? What's the difference between a dream you remember so vividly and an experience that only exists as a memory? Both cannot be touched, and yet both exist as products of the past that inevitably shape your future self. Sometimes I think a dream memory is just as important as anything we remember from our waking lives. Not to mention, of course, the strange dreams I had of the shaman, which allowed me to understand and do all types of things the real world would never have offered me.

In the end, it didn't matter. What did matter was the dream had unsettled me to the point I couldn't get back to sleep. Why did my mother have her face turned away from me, I wondered. I felt her rejection of me as a physical slap, and even now, that the dream was slipping into the past it still hurt. I kept going back over it, the way she refused to look at me a vivid image that just wasn't fading away.

I ended up tossing and turning for a couple of hours. Eventually, I got up. Great, I thought. This is my vacation, and it's been spent fighting monsters and making very difficult personal decisions. It was too early to go anywhere or do anything, so I ended up listlessly sitting in front of my computer, playing one of my favorite games. The lack of sleep and different threads running through my mind kept interfering with my game play, and I gave up in disgust, nothing was going right for me today, nothing.

I tried stretching out on the couch, hoping I could grab a nap. Sometimes I have insomnia, and it often helps if I try to sleep in a different situation. I lay stretched out for about half an hour, tossing and turning, trying to get comfortable. Mostly I was just trying to get my mind to slow down, to relax so I could drift off.

By this time, it was daylight, at least, and I could justify staying up. I decided it would be nice to go out for breakfast. A good restaurant was pretty close by, and a nice big meal sounded good. I found a table and ordered. I really like bone in ham steak with eggs, with home fries and toast. The coffee isn't really that good, but they offer free refills, so I could have all I wanted.

I felt a little better after breakfast and I paid the bill, and then turned away from the register to leave.

"Jim, is that you?" I heard a voice from behind me ask. I turned around and found myself face to face with Anne, the girl that I'd met at the trade show a few months ago.

"Oh, hey," I found myself mumbling, "I didn't know you lived around here."

"I like coming here every once in a while," she answered. "They have a really good breakfast."

I was confused and discomfited. She was really friendly, glad to see me. I remembered how she had blown me off after our "date", and I didn't quite know what to say.

She kind of wrinkled her nose. "Wow, you look like hell!" she exclaimed. "Is everything all right, are you okay?"

"Yeah, I'm all right," I answered, somewhat embarrassed. I had come down for breakfast unshaved, and without taking a shower. I hated the fact she had caught me in an unguarded state, when I was tired and with a lot on my mind.

Then I did something that I never do. I just couldn't understand why she was acting so friendly, not after our last encounter. I felt a little crazy anyway, so I just asked her.

"So why are you acting so glad to see me after blowing me off?"

"Blowing you off? What are you talking about?" she asked, her face suddenly somewhat wary.

"Yeah," I said, somewhat sharply. "I asked you out, you said okay, and then you show up with a couple of other guys. What was all that about?"

"Well Jim, since you asked," she flashed back, "when I meet someone and really don't know anything about them, I like to get to know them a little better in a situation where everyone can feel comfortable. I thought it'd be nice to do some climbing, then go out for a few drinks and relax, see how the rest of the night goes. Instead, you started acting all macho, and you didn't show any interest in talking to any of us. You never even acknowledged either one of my friends."

"You mean boyfriends," I shot back.

"No, just friends. We like hanging out. It's no big deal."

"Oh," I said, suddenly deflated. I had messed up.

Her eyes darted between my eyes and the rest of my face. Apparently, she was considering something mysterious.

After a while, she spoke.

"You know, when I met you, I thought you were a really cool guy. Then when we met at the wall you were completely different really obnoxious. You really need to lighten up, give people a chance to get to know you. Try making friends with someone and don't try to force it."

Then she reached out and touched me on the shoulder.

"Take care of yourself," she said and left.

I headed back home, my mind now even more muddled than before. I had misread her intentions, maybe she had really been interested in me. If so, I had messed up. That was the trouble with being awkward and having low social intelligence. Situations others are able to read and navigate with ease are indecipherable gibberish to me. Everyone in life has an IQ (intelligence quotient) and an SQ (social quotient.) Could these add up to a total quotient? What if all people have a total quotient that is about the same, and then it's just divided up into the two parts. If you happen to have a high IQ, you automatically have a low SQ. One thing for sure, it wasn't just me, the guys I work with all have high IQ's, and none of them could even remotely qualify as a people person.

I got back home, restless, and I didn't know what to do about it. I kept thinking about my encounter with Anne and how I'd misread the cues. I thought back to the little girl at the grocery store, how her mother had been so comfortable seeing her with me. I saw a fundamental aspect of myself. People like and trust me when they first encounter me. It was only later they would sometimes change their opinion. I felt a kind of shift taking place within, as if a very heavy ponderous set of gears were slowly moving from one track to another. I wanted to be this person others like and trust. I needed to rectify a major problem with that, though. I needed to go back out and get Audrey, while there was still time.

CHAPTER 22

The trip back out took forever. I kept trying to *will* the distance to shorten, to arrive. I was frantic inside my mind; worrying that I'd be too late, that Audrey would be dead. In my mind, I couldn't believe I had ever convinced myself taking her was a good idea. I felt I couldn't breathe and wouldn't be able to until I had her back in the Jeep and headed back home.

I continued on, pushing my speed up to nine over the posted limit. It should be okay, and it made me feel like I was doing all I could to get back to her as soon as possible. I let my mind wander as I drove, wondering what I was going to do once I had her back. After all, retrieving her was the right thing to do, and would serve to salve the gaping wound now open on my conscience, but it didn't solve the underlying issue.

I considered options, some of them crazy. I thought about some of the devices I use in my line of work to shield all types of things from unwanted electronic and electromagnetic signals. Shielded cables protected signals traveling from one place to another, but I didn't see how that would help. I needed to think bigger, to find an object to shield a human being, some type of box.

Then I had it. It was called a Faraday Cage. It worked by using certain materials to block incoming electromagnetic fields. The next question was, could I use it to block the signal between Coyote and Audrey? Was it an electromagnetic signal? Unfortunately, I thought not.

I didn't know where to find one of these cages anyway, but suddenly I had an idea. The spell of protection I had used to bring Audrey back had blocked Coyote from entering the cliff dwelling, forcing him to use a mere projection of his physical being to terrorize the shaman. It had somehow brought Audrey back into this world, probably by blocking the signal that kept a part of her in the place she had described to me.

I jumped a bit in my seat, and the Jeep wandered over the center stripe of the road, causing a long blaring horn blast to pop me back into awareness that I was driving. I corrected the Jeep and then cautiously thought about it a bit more. Unfortunately, I didn't have the ingredients with me. I had jumped in the car with nothing but the clothes on my back, determined to retrace my steps as quickly as possible. I just needed to go, grab the girl, and make it back to my townhouse as quickly as possible. I just hoped it wasn't too late and I would end up with Audrey on my conscience for the rest of my life. I was determined now; I wanted to make amends for leaving her. I was determined to save her, no matter the cost.

The trailhead came into view. Once again, the parking lot was empty, a spurned lover left alone and forever lonely, hoping to someday feel the warmth and joy of companionship. I parked the Jeep and didn't even bother locking it. I headed down the trail, half jogging and half running. Even though I was desperate to get back to the girl, I knew I had to carry her back. It wouldn't do any good to exhaust my energy on the trip out.

I reached the spot where I needed to leave the trail. I knew exactly where it was this time, no need to search. I zipped up the slight rise that gradually evened out into the little uplift of ground where Audrey would be. I rounded a small group of trees, searching in front of me for a glimpse of color. I slowed as I came closer, and then I saw a small flash of plaid shirt and blue jeans. She was still there! I knelt beside her.

It was as if she were dead. She was pale and unmoving, and she lay exactly as I had left her. I reached out to check for a pulse, when she moaned slightly. Her head shifted a bit, and her eyes fluttered open.

"Jim," she whispered. "You came back. Where did you go? Why did you leave me out here?"

I thought about coming up with an excuse or a lie, but then something inside of me stood up, and even thought it was difficult, I answered.

"I made a big mistake, Audrey. But I'm going to make it up to you now."

She didn't respond, and her eyes were closed again, her awareness once again ripped from this world and back to her battle with Coyote. I could sense her grip on the threads of her life, sometimes strong, and other times weak but always giving, never taking back. Any part of the seam ripped asunder couldn't be put back together, not while Coyote was at the other end, keeping a constant tension, always pulling, remorseless, relentless.

I slung her pack around my shoulder and then gathered her up. I turned and headed towards the path. I reached the Jeep without incident, and we headed back to where had started one day before.

CHAPTER 23

I carefully laid Audrey on the couch. I went back and made sure I had the chant memorized correctly. Once I was ready, I cast the spell of protection once again. If anything could build a wall around Audrey and sever the connection between this world and another, it was this. Soon I had all the ingredients—Snake, Bear, light, love, and food—to give the spell sustenance. It didn't take long, and I felt a vibration rippling through the air then come to a sudden end. I knew the spell was effective, and after catching my breath, I went over to Audrey.

I could see right away she was better. Some color had returned to her cheeks, and she rested quietly. I left her, not wanting to wake her, and went to get a bite to eat from the kitchen. I was finishing up and getting ready to wash the dishes, when I heard a noise from the living room. I went around the corner. She was sitting up on the couch. This was great news, and I hurriedly went over and sat down on the other end of the couch.

"How are you feeling?" I inquired. "You look a lot better."

"I feel better," she replied, "and a little hungry."

"Come in the kitchen. I'll fix you a meal," I gladly answered, heading back in.

I fixed her a hamburger and some fries out of a pack I keep in the freezer. I didn't know how much she remembered about the last couple of days, and so I didn't say anything, letting her eat and waiting to see if she'd ask me any questions. She finished the burger and fries, popping the last fry into her mouth after using it to swipe the last bit of ketchup off the plate.

"Thank you," she said.

"Oh, no problem. I'm just glad you're hungry. The spell worked, the connection between you and Coyote must be broken, and that's great news."

Audrey picked the fork up and then laid it back down.

A new expression troubled her face, the inward expression gone. She seemed to be totally of this world. For now, she was just a twelve-year-old girl.

"I can still feel the connection with Coyote. It's a lot better, but it's not gone. And it's already getting a little stronger. It's like the spell you used is wearing off." She grimaced with pain. "It's already starting to hurt again."

Then she turned away, and I could see her shoulders shaking. She was crying, and I moved towards her, trying to figure out a way to help.

Suddenly she turned and grabbed me, hugging me tightly, her head on my shoulder. My arms instinctively moved around her, and she sobbed.

"I don't want to die," she managed to gasp out, a torrent of naked fear and desolation pouring out of her. "I'm afraid and I don't even know where I'll go if I die now. I might go back to that place where Coyote is. I want to be with my family again."

I felt a lump growing in my throat, and I felt tears, unbidden and unwanted, come to my eyes. I felt her desperation, her terrible impotence in the face of forces to great for her to fight, and in brilliant unfading light, my defenses against her pain crumbled, and I let her in.

Between my own tears I spoke. "Don't worry." I soothed her, and I stroked her hair. "I'm going to help you."

I felt a resolution, a rightness, about who I was and who I wanted to be form within, and with either great courage, or great stupidity, I sealed my fate. I gently disengaged from her. I asked her the question I knew would set me on a path that might end in my own death. Nonetheless, I was ready to do whatever it took.

"Audrey," I said, "you sent Coyote to that world, to the place where he brings the crazy stuff he uses to terrorize and destroy?"

"Yes," she answered, "I sent him."

Okay, I thought to myself, and found myself nodding my head. "Can you send me too?"

"Yes," she said, a little doubtfully, "if that's what you want."

"I want," I replied. "Let's do this while the spell is holding, while you still have the strength. Let's do it now."

CHAPTER 24

I didn't know what it would be like. I didn't know what would work or what wouldn't. She said it was dark, would a flashlight work? How about a gun? Could I even bring anything with me? It's best to be prepared, just in case, so I took my pack and arranged it. I didn't figure I'd need any food or water, since Audrey had survived for a few months without it, but I packed a little bit of each just in case. The pistol, absolutely. What if I could just find Coyote and fill his hide with lead, and it would be over? It was probably too easy, but worth a shot. Then I took a large flashlight and a small one as well. I had a small holster that I attached to my belt and put the small one in. It would be easy to get to that way. I didn't know what else to take, but I decided on a knife and a small pair of binoculars. The field glasses were expensive and quite good at gathering light. Perhaps I'd be able to use them to spot my enemy before he noticed me and sneak up on him. I checked the pack once more, wondering what else I should bring, and gave up. It didn't matter how long I agonized. I just wouldn't know what I should have brought until I arrived.

I shouldered the pack and stood in the middle of the room. I gave Audrey a nod. "Let's do this," I said, somewhat doubtfully.

Audrey didn't reply; she just raised her arms and closed her eyes. I didn't feel anything, but some ropy tendrils rose from the floor in front of me. The tendrils grew, getting thicker, taller, and more numerous. It was as if they fed from the air itself, but I knew they were created by the girl sitting on the couch.

I panicked as the tentacles formed a cage about me. An impulse flooded through me, a last blind appeal at self-preservation. I wanted to slip out between the growing mass of ropy material. I wanted to run, run away, and never come back. I didn't, though; one thing about me is that when I say I'll do something, I tend to always do it. It isn't an ethical thing, at least not totally. I just feel it "lessens" me somehow to break my word. This actually causes me problems in my relationships with others. I automatically assume when another says they'll do something, they'll do it. We always base our assumptions of how another person will react on how we ourselves will react. Many times in my life another person has said, "Sure, I'll do it," and I blindly stood by, waiting for them to do so, just to figure out they didn't really plan on following through. I guess I'm just naive at a very fundamental level.

The tentacles thickened, and it was hard to see through them now. I felt a sudden sensation of being trapped; I felt like I couldn't breathe. A solid wall stood in front of me now; not solid and static but pulsating, moving back and forth as a tree limb might waver in a gentle breeze. The wall stiffened and then imploded on me. Suffocation, darkness. I was jerked down into the earth. I travelled through dirt and soil. I felt clods bursting about me, on me, in me. Then I was through, and the universe opened before me.

I was beyond space and time, and a river of stars lay before me, a narrow thread of light curving its way through the dark, much like a stream might meander through a field. All went black, and I landed, not gently, but solidly, on a hard surface. All was dark. I was on a street made of glass. Buildings lined each side of the street, some short, some impossibly tall. They were black, only distinguishable from the darkness around me by the fact they were even darker than night itself. Some of them glittered in the night but with darkness rather than light. I knelt and put my hand on the street beneath me. It was smooth, firm, and unyielding. Even though it was dark, I could see the buildings continuing on both sides of the street, out to the limits of my vision. To the right and to the left—it didn't matter; both ways were the same, indistinguishable from each other. I chose left at random, mostly because I'm left-handed, and sauntered off, wondering what I would do if I was able to find Coyote.

I strode down the street, the building slowly passing by, with changes in their height and configuration. I absently remembered my pack and checked for it. I did have it, and I reached down and pulled the small flashlight out of the holster. I turned it on but, much I suspected, it didn't work. I thought about trying my pistol but decided against it. If Coyote was here, and I could find him, it would be better if he didn't know I had it. I might even be able to shoot him before he knew I was here.

I continued down the street for a few minutes, or a few

years: I couldn't tell. After some time, I reached an intersection. The road I was on was similar to the one that stretched out from the night, right and left being just two more options that made no difference in this endless city of glass.

On impulse I took the left branch, continuing with the idea that maybe left was lucky, or better. The buildings continued to silently slide by me as I made my way through the silent streets. Out of curiosity and boredom, I walked over to one of the buildings. It towered over me, a vast, brooding monolith of indifference and casual authority. I placed my hand on the surface. It was the same smooth glass that made up the street: dark, impenetrable, and cold. An entrance to my right had a rectangular opening that was barely visible, a void against the smooth walls of the building. I went inside, wondering if I could climb up and get some type of perspective on the city. A stairwell sprang from my right, and it opened up into the rest of the building, beckoning me in a desultory fashion. It was broad and spacious, wide enough for half a dozen people side by side at least, and the ceiling above was high, almost invisible in the gloom that pervaded the interior.

I ascended, noticing that climbing required little effort. I didn't feel out of breath, or tired, and the levels in the building glided placidly by as I made my way up towards the top.

I reached the final floor of the structure, and the staircase ended at a large featureless room that extended the width and breadth of the entire construct. A huge open window spread across the wall that faced the street, a gaping maw that should allow an unrestricted view of the entire city. I ventured over, the size and shape of the window, coupled with the distance to the street below, giving me a brief feeling of vertigo and unease. I was concerned I might misjudge the edge of the building, the distinction between solid structure and open air a tenuous concept in this strange world. I approached a solid wall and kept a hand on it as I neared the edge of the building. I reached the end of the wall after a bit, and then I gathered myself and looked out at the vista spread below.

CHAPTER 25

The city lay before me, a startling juxtaposition of geometrical angles and lines. Everything was rigidly regular, no curves or unexpected angles. It was a world of ninety-degree angles, with buildings crashing into one another or ripped asunder with gaps in between. I couldn't see any variation, anything different, in the entire cityscape that lay beneath me. I took my time and scanned the entire area in front of me carefully.

I took out my binoculars and gave them a try. They worked okay. I was able to pick out a greater amount of detail and information in the buildings across the street. I used them to extend the far reaches of my vision. No change. The city didn't differentiate in any way as far as I could see, even with my binoculars. I heaved a sigh and returned the field glasses to my pack. I turned back to the stairway and as I approached the center of the room, I noticed a small window on the other side of the building. It was hard to make out, but the slight difference in texture of the wall made it possible. I decided to go over and check it out, hoping it might be more interesting on the other side of the city.

I didn't have to creep up to this one. It was much smaller and didn't give the same perspective of opening up to the universe. The window grew in size and shape as I grew closer, and I could tell it was about six feet square and located about three feet from the floor. It should be perfect for discovering what lay outside. It was the same viewpoint as the other side, an endless array of buildings of various sides, all perfectly rectangular in shape. I took the binoculars and slowly inspected the landscape in front of me, hoping to find an irregularity to check out.

I didn't think I'd find anything, but at the farthest reach of my vision, with the binoculars, I saw nestled between two skyscrapers, a pyramid. Huge and glistening with a primordial darkness, it gracefully formed a triangular shape, jarring the senses against all the sharp angles that formed the rest of the city. I felt a burst of excitement. At least this was unusual, different. I felt Coyote would probably be there, as surely, he would want to stay at a place that had some type of significance in this monotonous, predictable place.

I sighted in on it, trying to figure the angle from where I stood. I knew this place didn't really have any points of reference for planning a hike to a certain place, but I would make a best guess and then head in that direction.

CHAPTER 26

I made my way out of the building and back into the street. Then I got my bearings and headed back toward the intersection. The street to my left should lead in that direction. I wondered how to calculate distance in a world with no landmarks, and my body never got tired.

I decided to choose and enter one of the tall buildings I was passing at set intervals, or what I could guess to be set intervals. I noticed my sense of time was better now that I had a specific goal in mind. Maybe it was the sheer sameness of this place, the unending litany of streets and skyscrapers that made time so elusive, like a slippery bar of soap that just couldn't be grasped.

At last, the pyramid loomed closer, and I could see it was offset from the street, so anyone just passing by would never see it. I took a path between two of the buildings and came out into a large plaza. The pyramid squatted before me, resolute and powerful. I crossed the plaza and stood directly before it. I searched for an entrance, and I didn't see anything. The face of the pyramid was a blank expanse of featureless glass, unmarred by door or window. I decided to circle the entire base of the structure if necessary. I had to find an entrance. I took to the left again; it had worked so far and worked my way towards the corner that lay in the distance. I estimated this pyramid was around two hundred yards wide at the base, and while not as tall as it was wide, the peak still towered above me, a small mountain peak that was almost lost in the gloom.

I made it to the corner. All I spied on the other side was a continuation of smooth, dark glass. A small blemish in the otherwise unbroken line that made up the structure. Well above the level of the street, it was located about halfway down the side of the pyramid. I grew steadily nearer to the blemish, and it soon transformed into a set of steps leading up to an opening.

I found the entrance. I hurried up the steps, which were about six feet wide and soon found myself standing on a small platform, inset into the side of the edifice. A small arched tunnel led into the interior. It was about six feet wide and eight feet high, topped with a semicircle that formed the arch. I didn't see anything else, so I headed inside.

CHAPTER 27

The tunnel went for about a hundred feet, then opened into a large open area. The interior of the pyramid was open, and a small ledge about twenty feet wide snaked its way around the inside, trailing off into darkness both to my right, and left. I knew the area beneath me dropped off towards the base of the pyramid, because I could see the same happening on both sides, so the lower reaches were wider than the upper, the inside gradually narrowing to nothing as it approached the apex. I could see a curious area below me. Liquid pooled on the pyramid floor. I could see an area of greater darkness that extended in a large rectangle that made its way almost to the sides of the structure. A small pathway surrounded this pool on both sides, and I assumed this ran beneath where I stood as well. Small flashes of light occasionally burst in the liquid, vivid flashes of white, so incongruous against the twilight. These flashes came every few seconds, randomly throughout the pool, not really creating any light, just rousing my curiosity. I wanted to find a way down to the bottom of the pyramid.

I circled the platform around the pyramid at this level, choosing left again, didn't see any reason to change up now. As I made my way to the corner of the structure, the inner wall was as smooth and featureless as it had been outside. I reached the corner and turned right, the only possible option. I made it about halfway down the length of the path on this side. I wondered if I'd see anything different from this perspective.

The pool was exactly the same as where I'd entered. Below the entrance the walls slowly sloped outwards, just as they did in the rest of the structure. I couldn't see any doorways to the pool, but it was too far down to be sure in the persistent gloom. The flashes of white in the pool added to the difficulty with seeing any entranceways as well.

I continued my circuit, and when I reached the wall directly opposite of the outside entrance, I found it. A short tunnel led towards the exterior of the pyramid. I took it and found it went about fifty feet then opened into a hallway. From this hall were two staircases, one heading up and one heading down. I took the one heading down, hoping it would lead me to the bottom.

I zigzagged back and forth. The staircase was just like those in a building back home, one part heading toward the interior of the pyramid and then switching back toward the exterior. It didn't take long to get down, and soon I was on the bottom floor. A hallway similar to the one upstairs, and from of it, a tunnel led inside. *It should lead to the pool.* I anxiously set off, wanting to end my journey as soon as possible.

The tunnel opened onto the bottom floor, and the pool lay before me, just as I hoped it would. From the edge, the surface was a shimmering black skin devoid of all warmth. The lights were flashing, just as before, intermittently throughout the pool. One flashed near me, a pure white pulse of energy, about a foot long and an inch wide. Another burst close by, and I could see it was slightly curved rather than straight, and its edges were somehow "blurred." It was as if no definite boundary demarcated the pool and the energy.

I squatted down and reached out my hand toward the liquid. I moved slowly, carefully; in case it was not water. I barely touched the surface with the tip of the index finger on my right hand. The moment I made contact, I jerked back and waited to see what would happen. Nothing happened. It indeed was just water, or some other form of liquid that wasn't harmful. I watched the interplay of lights throughout the pool for a time, a few moments, or maybe much longer. The flashes exhibited quiet elegance, silently bursting with silvery light, and I felt a kind of sadness steal over me that I would never be able to share this beauty with any other person.

I snapped back into the reality of what I was here for and what I needed to do. I circled the pool, keeping an eye out for any other passages that might lead to another part of the pyramid. I traversed one side of the pool and then the entire length of another and made my way down the side opposite of where I had stood. In the center of the wall lay another tunnel, leading toward the outside of the pyramid once again.

I took it, and as I neared the outside wall, the passage once again opened; this time into a rectangular room. The room was alight with a dim greenish yellow glow that radiated from the floor and lit the room with a soft light that was stronger at the floor and then dissipated as it rose toward the ceiling. The top of the room wasn't far above my head. It was too close to the outside of the pyramid to be very high, and I saw another doorway off to my left, not far away at all.

Through the doorway I entered another small passage. I could see it ended at a shaft that rose into the upper levels of the structure. I approached the shaft and a small silver square floated slowly upwards on a journey to the unknown. I stopped at the edge of the duct. The shaft continued up into the nether reaches of the pyramid, a square duct made of dark bricks, cunningly interlocked with each other, and transforming seamlessly into the glass of the rest of the building. The tunnel was lit with the silvery white glow of the squares floating past. I saw one coming and reached my hand out into the shaft.

The square intersected my hand and dissolved softly, parting to float past the barrier my hand represented, and then forming into a whole unit once again on the other side and continued its path upward.

Memories. The thought came into my mind unbidden. The squares were memories. I reached out again, and as the square made contact, I felt a surge in my mind and a fleeting sensation of being on a trail. A young Native American girl was beside me, hand in hand. My hand was not really human, more of a hand-paw.

I must be Coyote, I mused to myself, a mixture of morbid curiosity and sick revulsion running through me as I experienced the world through his eyes. Then the memory broke, the contact severed, and the silvery white square continued its journey. It was composed of small, detailed images, a patchwork of periods in the life of a being that I was here to find.

I turned back away and made my way back to the main room. I turned to the left and found another doorway a small distance away. This one led to another stairway, much narrower than the others, only about four feet wide. I climbed the stairs, with heightened sense of urgency, mingled with fear. I really thought Coyote was close now. I pulled out my pistol and racked a shell into the chamber. I clicked the safety off and continued upward, step by step and level by level.

I reached another point where the stairway turned back on itself and zigzagged up to where an opening appeared before me. A light appeared in the opening, and it was strangely familiar, the warmth and welcoming of a light from home, yellow, normal, safe.

I eased forward in the dark, automatically sidling up to one of the walls, and continued climbing step by step.

The dark walls slowly melted into brick, the same as from the shaft below. I took one step at a time, pausing after each one, trying to get a view into the space above. I could see a bit of ceiling now, and I caught the beginning of walls. The ceiling was adorned with a huge chandelier, and the walls were hung with rich tapestries, red and blue, forming a startling contrast to the world I had seen up to now.

I advanced another step, and the room took shape. It was long and narrow, with various pieces of furniture, a couch and a couple of writing desks. The floor was festooned with carpets, various geometrical designs made me think of Byzantine artwork. I reached the final step and stood at the edge of the room. It was well lit, and not only showed signs of habitation but also "felt" like a room someone lived in. There was no sign of life though.

I checked out the various furnishings. The place was very comfortable, a nice place to live, especially considering the rest of this world. The desks were covered in papers, some of them containing elements hand-written but with a type of lettering system and language I'd never seen before. Various writing instruments were scattered, all of them antique pens, the type that require dipping in ink. A couple of inkwells were stationed on both desks.

One of the papers had a drawing on it, and I picked it up, curious. It was a scene from a primordial world, perhaps earth, a shape emerging from a blizzard, one that could slowly be discerned to be a mammoth. The curved tusks were clearer than the rest of the animal, two spiral, disembodied spirits, lost in the storm. The trunk and face were visible, although the detail was already beginning to fade, the victim of the remorseless snow. The rest of the animal was just a vague suggestion of shape, a delicate hint I could barely make out from the blizzard. The drawing was amazing; not only capturing detail, but also evoking emotion, and I gave a small gasp of pleasure at the beauty and feeling of loss the drawing evoked in me.

"It's one of my favorite memories," came from behind me.

I jumped, and almost lost the grip on the gun, the sound of the voice sending a shock through my whole body. I turned and saw Coyote standing about ten feet away from me in the middle of the room.

"What do you mean, memories?" I asked carefully, trying to assess the best way of proceeding. *Should I shoot him now or wait and try to get some information out of him first?*

"I've got lots of time, now that I'm stranded here for the time being," he continued, "so I'm going through some of my old memories, and getting rid of a lot of the ones that are; should I say "forgettable"?" He chuckled.

"Certain ones I cherish I'm drawing out and putting into the system; that way, no matter what I'll have them. The time I saw the mammoth coming out of the blizzard—wow, it was just so beautiful, so awe inspiring. Even I, a god, felt small, when I saw him."

"Of course, some of the other ones I treasure for different reasons. If you don't mind," he said, eyeing the gun pointedly, "I'll show you."

I was fascinated despite myself, and so, even though I knew it was stupid, I nodded my head for him to continue.

He sauntered over to a door situated between two wall hangings. The door was wood and it could have been at home in any custom built, expensive home. He opened it, and gestured for me to come over, grinning at me when he saw how carefully I made my way across the room to a point where I could get a good angle but making sure to leave plenty of space between us.

Coyote graciously stepped aside so I could get a good view. Inside was a small opening that accessed the shaft I had seen below. As I watched one of the squares floated by, and I realized what it was.

"These are your memories?" I queried.

"Yes," Coyote nodded. "This is where I can add one whenever I get finished. I can also pull one out to edit if I feel like it. For example."

At this he grabbed a lever and manipulated a large piece of what appeared to be glass out into the stream floating by. The next square came up and softly affixed itself to the glass. Coyote extended another lever, and another piece of glass went out. He pushed, and the two pieces of glass came together, sandwiching the memory in between. He pulled it out of the stream, and I could see it became nothing more than a piece of paper as it lay outside the shaft. He opened the glass and took it out.

"I think you saw this one a while ago," he grinned at me. "It's one of my favorites."

"Who was that girl?" I blurted out unconsciously.

"Her name was Breela," he said. "She was a very special girl to me. I really enjoyed feasting on her bones. You see, she was the daughter of a man who was a real pain in the ass. He was almost as bad as you and that bitch, what's her name, Audrey?"

Shaman's daughter, the one in the vision. I realized with horror that I had seen a memory of Coyote leading her away, just before he finished her.

"I'm going to enjoy putting you and her in there too." He growled softly, gesturing to the duct. "Maybe I should just bring her down here right now," he said, making a yanking motion in front of him.

I felt an instinctive desire to just shoot him and get it over with, but I also felt cautious. I mean, if I could really just shoot him, then why was he acting so confident? And what was he talking about when he mentioned bringing Audrey down right now? What was he doing with his hands? I could see out of Coyote's stomach, heading up through the ceiling of the room, a small greenish yellow line. It was so light I almost didn't notice it, and it seemed to be composed of energy. This was the tether, the link between Audrey and him; this is what I needed to somehow cut.

Coyote watched me intently, obviously enjoying my indecision. He seemed willing to give me all the time I needed to decide what to do.

I decided. Surely if he was dead, the link would dissolve, and Audrey would be free. Then she could use her power to bring me back, and all would be well. At least that was the hope.

I slowly, deliberately brought up the pistol and centered it on him. Coyote didn't do or say anything, just continued grinning balefully. *Maybe he's just trying to psyche me out, bluff me.*

In any case, I didn't see what else to do. I fired, making sure to keep the pistol steady. The hole appeared in the middle of his chest, and he gasped and bent over. He didn't go down though, and I panicked and fired the rest of the magazine into him, little holes appearing in his chest and head, where he was bent over.

Time stood still, even in a place like this where time is already askew, and I felt I was frozen. The light from the chandelier flickered. I saw the oscillations in frequency as electricity coursed through the hundreds of tiny bulbs. A great rushing sound went through the room, a wind that could rob death of warmth and courage, and Coyote slowly toppled to the floor, onto his face.

I went over to him slowly and reached out with my foot, giving his head a dubious nudge. He didn't move, and I knelt and stared at the holes in his back, furrows created by the bullets from my gun, gouging and tearing their way through his body. I felt a brief shadow of sadness and pity as I gazed upon him and wondered how many thousands or millions of years he had lived.

I was waiting for Audrey to bring me back. Surely it shouldn't take her long, now that she was free. I paced along the wall hangings and other furnishings, wondering how Coyote had managed to bring them here. I glanced over at his body from time to time, making sure it was still there. After a bit I got impatient and worried, and I sat at one of the desks, ruffling through the papers. Some of them had the strange writing, and others were partial drawings, the beginning of memories. One in particular caught my eye.

It was a drawing of Coyote, lying on a floor. The angle was very similar to how Coyote was lying now. Dread and doubt wrenched me. A small line was drawn very lightly, coming out of his midsection and angling towards the top of the drawing. I had missed it at first. The drawing suggested Coyote had seen and drawn this already and the link between him and Audrey still existed, even though he was dead.

Suddenly I jumped up from the desk and turned back towards the part of the room where Coyote lay. As I whirled around, I felt a firm hand-paw grip my shoulder, and I tensed, a feeling of inevitability coursing through me as I turned toward Coyote, only a few inches away.

Charles Combee

CHAPTER 28

"Sorry, Jimmy my boy," he said pleasantly. "It was a nice try, but you see, things just don't work like that around here. Now on earth…" he paused meaningfully, "this could have put a pretty good hurting on me, at least for a bit. Not here though."

I didn't know what to do, and I was petrified by fear. His waffling back and forth between pleasantries and incipient violence was just a way of squeezing every drop of terror he could out of me before he killed me. I didn't see any path in front of me now. I guess I should just hope he'll make it quick.

Coyote was obviously enjoying playing with me, and he put his arm companionably around my shoulder and led me over to the door with the memories. "Let's take a look at a couple more of these," he said, grinning at me. "I think you'll like them." He dexterously added the one square with Breela back into the stream, the square of paper transforming into a pale white wisp that slowly floated out of sight in the stream going by. Coyote watched the stream carefully, letting a couple of captured thoughts go by, and then he sighed.

"Ahhh, there we go, that's a good one." He reached in, just like a cook might reach into an oven to pull out a tasty confection and pulled out another recollection. "Here you go, try this one on for a size," he said helpfully, handing the square of paper to me.

I reached out dully, wondering what kind of carnage or rapine the paper would show me. I held it so the image was facing me. I was puzzled by the image of the shaman. He was showing his compassion and sympathy for my plight with his eyes, and I wondered why. I didn't quite understand why, strangely, the shaman came alive in the drawing and winked at me. He beckoned with his hand to come closer, and I instinctively pulled the paper towards me. Then he mouthed, in perfect English, so plainly I could read his lips: *death is just another journey.* Then he winked again, and suddenly the drawing changed into one completely different.

It was a woman, a hiker. She was dead, but I recognized her

from the news. She was the woman from the couple who had disappeared in the spring, just before I went out and found Audrey. Her body was covered in rips and tears, rough and jagged, as if they came from a saw, or more likely, teeth and claws. She was clad in a pair of panties, soaked in blood. This was where Coyote had gotten the underwear he had used to terrorize me. This is why he wanted me to see this particular drawing.

I handed it back to him, saying nothing. He waited, suspiciously, obviously expecting a reaction, disgust or fear.

"You know who that was, don't you?" he ventured.

"I know," I replied. "It doesn't really matter now, though, does it?"

He grinned at me, but I could still see he was thinking, considering. Then I could see he had made up his mind.

"I guess it's time," he said, "time for you, me, and Audrey to be together, together forever. Don't worry, Jimmy boy," he said, "it'll be fun; we can have contests, play games."

"Games," I said. "What are you talking about?"

"Oh, you know," he winked at me. "I can torture both of you and the one who screams the loudest will be the winner. You know, stuff like that." He grinned at me with obvious relish.

I wasn't sure what was going on, but I knew I needed time. I needed to understand what the shaman was trying to tell me. I knew Coyote didn't know what had happened, and it had to be important, I just needed to figure it out.

"Maybe we'll torture you instead," I shot back, being awkward on purpose. "Maybe the one who makes you scream the loudest will be the winner."

Coyote laughed, and I got the feeling he really thought it was funny. "You know, Jimmy boy," he said, "I actually do like you. It'd be a shame to get rid of you; you're a lot of fun."

"Okay," I responded slowly, one side of my mind engaged on answering him, the other trying desperately to figure out what the shaman was trying to tell me. "In that case why don't you just let Audrey go? Since I'm so much fun, I should be all the entertainment you need."

"Not a chance of that, I'm afraid," he responded icily. "That little bitch pissed me off, and I want her ass down here too. You know, I can bring her down here anytime; all I have to do is yank on this," he grabbed the tether going out through the roof meaningfully, "really hard, and she'll come tumbling down."

"You know," he mused suddenly. "I remember tumbling down from somewhere else. Hmmm, what was that?" He put his paw-hand up to his elongated chin, seemingly lost in thought. "Oh yeah, I remember now, it's a book a kid had a while back about nursery rhymes. Jack and Jill. You know, it was actually a pretty good book. I kind of liked it."

Tumbling down. I was obsessed with this idea. Tumbling down was important.

Then I had it. I understood. Shaman had explained it. *Death is just another journey.* I was going to have to die to get out of here.

CHAPTER 29

I thought frantically, trying to decide what to do and how to do it. Unfortunately, I had used all my bullets on Coyote, so the pistol was useless. I had to figure another way. Tumbling down, tumbling down, it kept coming to my mind. I could run for the stairs and try to "tumble" down them, but Coyote would probably catch me before I even landed. On the other hand, maybe he would just kill me; it was worth a try. I faded into a martial arts move and aimed a kick at his head. Coyote dodged me easily, a quizzical expression on his face.

"Let's just fight it out," I said, "you and me, to the death. May the best man win."

With a withering tone to his voice Coyote said, "That's not going to happen, Jimmy boy, not going to happen. I'm going to be trapped here for a long time. Not forever, mind you, but for a while. And I'm keeping you around for entertainment. So, you might as well just settle in for the long haul. You, me, and Audrey, we're just going to be one big happy family!"

I felt a brief flare of disappointment and dread. No telling how many different ways he could figure to hurt, frighten, and torture me without killing me. Death would be a blessed relief; if I could get it.

Then I had an idea, one that might work. "So, how do those squares of paper change into those misty, cloud like things?" I asked about the shaft. "Is it magic?"

"It's only magic if you don't understand how it works," he replied, but I could see he was pleased. "I just think the paper into another form. Kind of like how I thought one of your smart phones into working or thought a fragment of internet into the cave I used to live in down in the canyon. Oh," he suddenly mused, "that's right, you didn't realize how I kept tabs on you, did you? Yeah, it was fun, learning about all that stuff." Then he winked at me. "That's what happens when you go up against a god, you know, you lose."

"So, can I watch you do it again?" I queried, ignoring his superior attitude.

"Yeah, why not," he responded. "After all, we've got plenty of time, if you know what I mean."

Then he entered the room where the memories were floating by. I crowded in beside him, desperately hoping he'd think I was fascinated by the process. He peered into the shaft, looking for a good bloody one no doubt, and I sidled up and glanced down. The shaft went clear down to the floor below, a good fifty feet or so. The squares slowly floated up and I wondered how a being so cruel and terrible could create such beauty. I thought about the memory of the mammoth, and inside myself I shook my head.

Then without warning I jumped into the stream.

I heard Coyote howl behind me, and I was plummeting towards the floor. I closed my eyes, the fear of dying overcoming me, even though I knew it was the only way out. I waited for a second, expecting…I don't know what, but nothing happened, and I opened my eyes.

The stream was slowing me down, and I floated down the shaft, memories wafting their way around me, splitting into various nebulous pieces and rejoining after I had passed by.

I had plenty of time to plan and I was ready the moment the stream gently deposited me on the floor. I took off running. I didn't know where Coyote was, but I knew I needed to figure out another way of dying. I headed back for the pool and flashed into the tunnel leading from this smaller room into the main area of the pyramid. I sailed into the main area and dove into the pool, jumping as far as I could out into the dark water.

I knew this was going to do the trick because I didn't know how to swim.

The water took me in, as a lover might take one into her warm embrace. I sank rapidly, and I knew I was going to die now. Even though I wanted this on a conscious level, the will to live is strong, and I floundered, desperately striving to make it to the surface of the water. A breath of air was all I could think about, and I blindly gasped, taking in water rather than life giving oxygen.

I would give anything; do anything, for just one more breath of life.

It didn't matter though, because the only thing I could find was water. I took another breath, and the water came into my lungs. It hurt terribly, and I felt the strings, the sinews that held my life together within me, start to unravel.

The flashing lights approached. Slowly but surely, they came and surrounded me. As I drifted away, they took form and substance. The shaman greeted me. He smiled and held out his hand, and I took it. Then Snake appeared, and Bear, both greeting me as a brother. I wondered for a moment why I had ever been afraid, and I rejoiced in the knowledge of my death.

Shaman pointed behind me. In the water, not far from me, was a being. Composed of orange and yellow light, it burned, lighting the water with a cruel flame that spread throughout the water. This was Coyote. I was seeing him from the perspective of death.

What before would have been impossible was now easy. I drifted over to him and located the shining tendril of energy that linked him and Audrey. I grasped it firmly, placing my feet against Coyote's stomach to get more purchase, and then I pulled. The tendril was rooted deep, just like a stubborn weed in a field, and I gritted my teeth and pulled harder. I worked the tendril back and forth, using my knowledge of growing up on a farm to good advantage.

The tendril slowly loosened, and I worked it back and forth faster. As I struggled with it, it finally broke free, and came out of Coyote with an explosion of light and despair. Audrey was free. I could see the roots wriggling, trying desperately to get inside to the fertile ground that was Coyote. I hesitated for a moment, and then with sudden assurance I released the tendril. It immediately shot toward the ceiling and disappeared from my sight and this world and back to Audrey.

My task was complete, and I drifted through the water. Shaman, Bear, and Snake all stood before me, then another appeared. It was Breela, and she joined Shaman shyly, reaching for his hand with her smaller one. He took her hand and smiled at me. Then, after one last moment of togetherness and sharing, they turned and swiftly transformed back into flashes of light, joining the others in the vast lake.

I didn't know what to do now, and so I slowly drifted in the lake, not knowing what was next, or if this was my place forever. I didn't know if I was dead, and this was where I would remain forever or not.

I thought about my physical body which I knew was still on the couch back on earth. It seemed an abstraction at best, and I knew my physical form didn't really matter, that nothing else mattered.

I continued on for a bit and I realized the lights were gone. The lake suddenly went dark, then disappeared.

CHAPTER 30

I woke up on the couch and tried to get my bearings. Audrey sat in a chair next to the couch, watching me. Her eyes were clear; it was as if she were "here", all the way.

I heaved myself up and shook my head, trying to clear the cobwebs, to understand that it was really over, that I was back in my house and Coyote was gone.

"How long have I been back?" I muttered, half to myself and half to Audrey.

"About an hour," she answered. "You were really out of it, so I let you sleep."

"So…what happened?" I ventured.

"I'm good," she replied. "Better than I have been for a long time."

"And Coyote?" I asked warily.

"I'm clear of him. You were gone about an hour, and then suddenly I felt as if a fire had flared in my stomach. It hurt for a bit, but then I felt better, much better. I brought you back as soon as I could. It didn't take long; I knew where to find you."

"So that's it, then. We're free, wow. I'm lost, not having to fight or worry about some evil creature coming after me."

"I know what you mean," Audrey replied, looking at me expectantly.

"So, what now?" I asked simply.

She hesitated for a moment, as if unsure how I would react, but then she told me what she wanted to do.

I agreed, and so we made preparations and headed out.

CHAPTER 31

I pulled the Jeep up to the trailhead, once again parking at a now familiar spot. Audrey was in the passenger seat, her pack snugly resting on her lap. The expression on her face as we pulled up was almost, but not quite, one of peace.

I shut off the engine, awkwardly got out, and went over to passenger side. I gently opened the door. Audrey stepped out, bringing her pack with her. I watched as she adjusted it on her back, getting it set at the right spot.

"Are you sure this is what you want?" I asked quietly.

The inwardness was gone, and once again she was a twelve-year-old girl. She smiled at me, in such a way that I felt naïve and innocent beside her.

"I miss my mom and dad," she said simply. "I even miss Timmy, most of the time, anyway. I want to be with them again."

"Okay," I said. "Would you like to get my number, just in case?"

"Sure, why not," she said, and took out her phone.

"It's five-five-five-zero-two-one-three," I offered, watching as she deftly put the numbers in.

"Must be nice not to have to worry about things like battery power left, signal strength, and data left on your plan," I observed.

"Yeah, it's all right," she said smoothly. "At least I got that much out of this whole experience."

"If you ever get tired, or lonely, just call and I'll come get you."

"I know," she said, "thanks."

Then she raised her hand. "Bye," she said, and turned and headed down the trail, towards the canyon.

I watched her for a few minutes, as she moved easily along the trail, her figure slowly getting smaller as she moved farther away. Finally, she topped a small rise and disappeared on the other side. I went back to the Jeep, turned the ignition, and headed back to town, and the life that waited for me.

As I drove back to the city, my townhouse, and my life, I reflected on all that had happened in the last week and whether any of it meant anything, in the end. The one thing that kept popping up was my chance meeting with Anne. Not only had it helped me make a decision that would shape who I was and how I felt about myself for the rest of my life, but it had given me an insight into how I relate to others and what they see me.

I had always been so goal-oriented, so determined to get a date, a girlfriend, anything as long as I could be like everyone else. Now I understood I had completely overlooked the idea of friendship and giving others an opportunity to get to know me. No wonder I had so much trouble meeting someone.

Even though I was no different in many ways now than I was a week ago, I had a valuable understanding of myself, and by extension, people around me.

Did this really change anything right now? No, it did not. I would still pass many weekends lonely and bored, because I am just not that person that goes out and is always surrounded by friends. The important thing was that I no longer wanted to be that person, I preferred to be myself, even though it was the more difficult path.

I knew of no guarantees in life, it was possible I might never meet the right "one." Not all people do, you know.

However, I was determined to begin living differently; I wanted to squeeze all the joy and happiness I could out of life, just like getting that last drop of orange juice out of a juicer. I wanted to live and appreciate what I have. And no matter what, to accept I have value as a person, and fitting in isn't a requirement to live a good life.

Coyote had given me this much, and in a way, I guess I owed him, just a little bit.

Caracal, Romania-Albuquerque New Mexico-Clinton, Utah-Colombo, Sri Lanka

ABOUT THE AUTHOR

Charles Combee was born in southwest Colorado, where he learned to love hiking and enjoying the great outdoors. An inveterate traveler, he has lived and worked in different countries throughout the world. *Coyote* is his first novel.

Maya, Resurrected – Kimberly Todd Wade

859 A.D. Yohl Ik'nal ("Heart of the Wind Place") is alone with her two starving children on their drought-stricken farm. Her husband and two grown sons have been drafted to fight in a distant war. Will they ever return? Yohl can't afford to wait. Her hungry children must be fed. It's time to dig up Yohl's past, for her mother was a princess, her grandfather a king. She still has relatives amongst the Maya royalty. They are her best hope for salvation.

Follow Yohl and her children as they travel Maya causeways, highways of the ancient world, through ravaged jungle and depressed homesteads to the capital city, itself on the verge of economic collapse.

Can the religious spectacle of human sacrifice provoke the Gods' beneficence? If the Maya ceremonies and myths fail, Yohl has recourse to the older, deeper traditions of the forest people.

She'll do whatever necessary to survive.

Seventh Daughter – Ronnie Seagren

Some people are destined from birth to do great things.

Gil Orlov is born in the shadow of totality of a solar eclipse, the seventh daughter of a seventh daughter. She is the culmination of a carefully planned genealogy begun by her great-grandmother. Gil's purpose, the goal of her family—defeating a Vision of the world in flames, reduced to a lifeless cinder.

But the power she should have is muted or lacking. Gil and her six sisters begin an arduous journey to a place of power high in the Peruvian Andes known as Killichaka—the Bridge to the Moon. They must make it to this ancient temple in time to complete a ritual during the totality of the 1937 solar eclipse. If they are successful, Gil's powers should be restored—giving her the ability to prevent the global disaster her ancestors warned of.

To succeed they must first survive the journey and locate Killichaka. Against them is the environment, the elements, their own doubts and fears as well as the 'Other' and a force that would gleefully see the world fall into chaos—an entity known as Supay.

Small-g City – S.D. Matley

Seattle is on the brink of disaster, but nobody knows it! Nobody except Ralph, a "small-g" god from Olympus, Inc.

Ralph suffers from extreme job burn-out, and no wonder— his job is to reinforce Seattle's notorious raised highway, the Alaskan Way Viaduct, by disbursing his molecules throughout the unstable and hazardous structure.

But Ralph's molecules are feeling the pull of reconstitution. Will he survive one more agonizing rush hour without resuming his humanoid form and emerging from the viaduct, sending thousands of commuters to their deaths? And what about the familiar shadow hovering over him? If Zeus (Olympus, Inc. CEO and the Biggest of Big-G Gods) is spying on him, all Tartarus is sure to break loose!

Big-G City – S.D. Matley

Veronica Zeta, youngest child of Zeus and Hera, is at last CEO of the immortal owned and operated corporation, Olympus, Inc. The biggest project on her agenda is creating world peace, but first she must depose her bloodthirsty brother Ares, God of War. To do so, she must deploy a supernatural force called The Power, which can demand a terrible price.

Zeus, former CEO and Ex-Lord of the Universe, struggles with identity issues after his retirement. The bright spot in his life is babysitting his toddler granddaughter, but his marriage with Hera is foundering and he longs for someone to confide in.

Hera's new campaign, a mortal lifestyle series of books and seminars called Marvelous Marriage, is a huge success. The face of this project, small-g goddess Candy Smith, has become a media celebrity. Hera, Goddess of Marriage, revels in the market share she's stealing from the "adult" industries owned by her rival, Aphrodite.

But Aphrodite, Goddess of Love, is ready to fight back! Employing a photo-shopped tabloid cover photo and a box of enchanted chocolates, she disrupts the personal life of Candy Smith and goads Hera into executing her own sabotage plan.

The lives of these Olympians collide when Veronica succeeds in deposing Ares, and pays for deploying a large dose The Power with blindness, anguish and, possibly, death. But how can an immortal die? The answer lies in an old family secret, daringly unearthed by Zeus in the eleventh hour.

Beyond Big-G City – S.D. Matley

The year is 2025 and Hermes is on the Olympus, Inc., hot seat. He has two short years to halt climate change before the irretrievable tipping point is reached, an existential threat to mortals and immortals alike.

David Bernstein embarks on a quest to learn about his unnamed mortal father. Assisted by would-be girlfriend, Cleo Petra, David scours the Middle East for clues that lead him to Rome, Italy, and points beyond.

Jim Smith observes unsettling changes in Stella, his mental health client, and fears an evil force, The Power, has secretly escaped its prison to terrorize the City of Mount Olympus once more.

And what of Seattle? Clifford Essex leads a desperate race to solve the riddle of an unstable seawall, poised to crumble and take a major transit tunnel with it.

From Mount Olympus to the Underworld, from Petra, Jordan, to Seattle, Washington-much is afoot *Beyond Big-G City!*

Find out more about these and our other books at
www.wolfsingerpubs.com

Made in United States
North Haven, CT
10 March 2023

33897179R00085